MW00477131

Confessions
of the Antichrist

(A Novel)

ADDISON HODGES HART

Confessions
of the Antichrist

(*A Novel*)

Angelico Press

For information, address:
Angelico Press
169 Monitor St.
Brooklyn, NY 11222
angelicopress.com

ISBN 978-1-62138-515-8 (pbk)
ISBN 978-1-62138-516-5 (cloth)
ISBN 978-1-62138-517-2 (ebook)

Cover Design: Michael Schrauzer
Cover Image: Michael Schrauzer, Untitled Landscape
ca. 1983, acrylic on panel

Where there is great doubt
there will be a great awakening:
no doubt, no awakening.

(A Zen proverb)

I

THE night before I was abducted I had a dream.

In my dream I found myself in a foreign city, one that reminded me somewhat of Prague, but Prague as it had been in Soviet times. It was a gray day and I was out in the street in a rundown, seedy part of town. Every building's facade appeared to be streaked red-brown with rust. Lurid veins of corrosion ran down dun-colored and yellowing stucco walls amid the peeling and chipping of faded paint. There were rusty drainpipes, rusty manhole covers, rusty automobiles parked along the lanes, and there was rubbish strewn everywhere.

My mood was as dismal as my surroundings. I was distraught, shaken with anxiety, because I was being pursued, chased by a being I knew to be appallingly and terrifyingly malevolent. This evil entity, I knew, was intent on doing me some unthinkable harm.

The narrow, cobblestoned streets were a tangled maze and unfamiliar to me, and no matter which avenue I turned into and dashed down to elude my relentless pursuer, it always looked to me to be exactly like the one I had just left. Panic seized me. I was lost. What's more, there was with me a golden-haired woman, of whose safety I felt protective. She was no one I knew from my waking life, and yet I knew this woman in my dream and that she was precious to me, and that she had to be shielded from our pursuer as much as myself.

We were frantically running through streets and alleyways, and I was constantly looking back, glimpsing features of the creature that startled me—confused impressions of a

1

sweeping cape, black-gloved hands, the wings of a bat, and sometimes he even appeared to be gliding after us. With each backwards glance, I saw that he was gaining on us. He would soon overtake us if I couldn't find some way to dodge him. Once or twice I saw his face—a face handsome and unsettling at the same time. Years ago I had seen the actor Louis Jourdan in the role of Dracula in a television drama, and it was unmistakably *that* face that I now saw grimly and intently bearing down on us in my nightmare.

I desperately fled down the streets with this woman and somehow (I can't remember precisely how) we procured a motor scooter. We were suddenly streaking wildly down the lanes, our hearts racing at an even faster pace, and—after what seemed a very long and anxious stretch of time—we found ourselves on a long, narrow pier, buzzing frantically out towards its end and the vast ocean beyond. There, at the end of the pier, we abandoned our stolen scooter and, cornered, we awaited our fate.

But now we were no longer on a pier at all, but instead were on the summit of a huge trash heap, pressed up against a rust-brown chain-link fence, with nowhere to flee. Our pursuer glided steadily and triumphantly towards us, and, as he did, my fear mounted.

But then something extraordinary happened; the entire course of the dream changed and seemed to start flowing in the opposite direction. All at once, I felt an interior rush of energy rise up within me, and with it a new determination to turn around and confront our nemesis. Motioning my companion back, I moved forward and headed directly towards this embodiment of evil with Louis Jourdan's face. I no longer felt any dread. Instead, in its place, I felt an overwhelming sympathy and compassion for this creature. And my feelings went even further than that. I reached out with both my arms to embrace him. Faced with the prospect of that embrace, he began to shrink back in horror and to gibber incoherently. Then, as we watched, he shrank back whimpering, doubled over, then dwindled and withered and—like a blackened and blistering piece of burning paper caught up by the breeze—he was blown away in scattering ashen fragments in the air.

At that precise moment I awoke. Throughout the remainder of that day, this dream stayed with me. It seemed to me to be greatly significant, a portent of some kind, and I couldn't shake the lingering ominous impression it made on me. Was my unconscious mind trying to tell me something? I wondered. And why did the nightmare still preoccupy and trouble my thoughts a full twelve hours after I had dreamed it?

It was the events subsequent to my abduction that helped me make some sense of that dream, but that wouldn't come until much later, after much experience and much reflection. And how to connect the two rationally, much less explain it to you, isn't easily done even now, because reason itself in my case has been stretched to nearly the breaking point. But I see I've gone ahead of myself and need to go back and begin again. It's my task here merely to give an account of what I've been through and what led me to reach the point where I am now.

In fact, I owe you some explanations. As you are aware, I never reached the Nobel ceremony to deliver my speech and receive the Peace Prize last year, which caused such a great deal of scandal for everyone involved. No doubt you have wondered what happened. That needs to be explained truthfully. Many rumors need to be put to sleep and only I can provide the facts.

Also I must explain how it came to be that, during the same period, it was divulged to me that I was *chosen* and—unknown to me—*groomed* by a secret force behind the scenes to assume the position of the most powerful leader on earth. And last, I must tell you what my next course of action will be—a course of action that will inevitably have ramifications for us all.

My account here begins with the kidnapping, which was so carefully plotted and ingeniously executed that I believe it could never have been foreseen or prevented by anyone. Before coming to that incredibly well-executed operation, however, it seems right I should give you a brief review of certain details of my life.

Most of you know my biography. It's well documented, after all. You have very likely followed my life and career through books and the popular media for decades. My shadow has fallen across your lives, my face has been on your screens daily and on the front pages of newspapers and magazine covers worldwide, and there has been no place on the internet where you could completely avoid me. For that, no doubt I should apologize, but the culpability for that intrusion isn't really mine alone to bear.

The noteworthy facts of my life are these: I was born in Baltimore. I formed a major corporation by the time I was thirty, headquartered formerly in Albuquerque, but now in New York, which is dedicated to using advanced computer technology in the "War on Terror"—the shrewdly named "Systems Networking And Research Corporation," a name which says absolutely nothing about our real business of highly effective tactical death-dealing, and has a winsomely whimsical acronym (SNARC). I was (briefly) appointed President of the World Bank; became (again, briefly) the Secretary-General of the United Nations; and most recently I completed two very successful terms in the White House as President of the United States. The last genuine news about me that you heard was, no doubt, that I was preparing to embark on a trip to Oslo late last year in order to receive the Nobel Peace Prize, and then I failed to appear and was nowhere to be found. I was, of course, an unlikely choice to receive the prize; but, then, so had been Kissinger, who in turn had always served as a model for me of diplomacy—and, frankly, of ruthlessness when called for. What you know about me, given my CV, I'll be bold enough to say, should have earned for me a measure of your trust. I believe you will agree that I have previously shown myself to be a rational, astute, and sane man, unapologetically a pragmatist and a practitioner of the art of *realpolitik*. That is to say, someone who has gotten the job done, whatever the job has demanded.

So I will grasp the nettle at once and tell you flatly what will, I'm sure, alarm you. There is no easy or simple way to tell you what I am about to tell you, and your first impulse, when you have heard it, will be to think I have lost my mind. In your place, that's unquestionably how I would respond myself. All I can do, then, is appeal to your previous impressions of me and to suspend, at least until you have heard me out, your disbelief. So, here it is: I have it on excellent authority that I have been destined from ages past to take up the role of the "Antichrist"—that personage most feared and dreaded for millennia, foretold by prophets and seers, the one designated by such numerals, terms, and titles as "666," the "son of perdition," the "Beast," and so on. I know that that admission is startling. It startled me at first, and it still startles me when I focus on it. But I ask you to hold on and continue reading before dismissing my words outright. I have had that remarkable secret disclosed to me, as I say, on very good authority, and I have no reason—not after all I have been through since my abduction—to doubt it. Asking you to believe it, of course, is quite another matter.

But for the sake of argument and for old times' sake, please hear my story through. I will recount it as matter-of-factly as I can, and then you must judge. You may well walk away and continue to believe that I've lost my mind. I sympathize with you if you should take that attitude. But I am asking you for the moment just to hear my story to the end, to bear with me and not to throw this book of honest (honest in my mind, whether I'm deluded or not) confessions away—not yet, at any rate. Play along with me, humor me, but do hear me out. If you persevere, you may come to reevaluate the matter and consider that my assertion to be the Antichrist holds no real threat to any of you or to the world at large. I assure you that—whatever horrors you may attach to that name, assuming you allow that such beings as the Antichrist and the devil might conceivably exist—I am benign. So, for now, please just set aside your incredulity and restrain any repugnance at the name of Antichrist. It's only a name, after all.

II

ANYONE who has occupied the sort of important public positions I have cannot simply go off to a local barbershop whenever he needs a trim. So it is that I employed a personal barber to come to me. This barber's name was Vic, and I saw Vic once every week, excepting vacation times and holidays, over the span of a decade. He was, I was informed when we hired him, a New Yorker of Italian ancestry and a former Navy Seal. His features were gaunt; one might even say they were just this side of cadaverous. He was slender, tall, pale, black-haired, all angles and bones. In temperament, however, there was nothing deathly about him. On the contrary, he was good-natured, though serious, occasionally ebullient, but never too talkative, and he was clearly highly intelligent. He was a great reader of the classics, including Dante— whom, he was proud to inform me, he read in the original. And he was, most importantly, or so it seemed at the time, proficient with sheers and razor. He never nicked me even once in ten years. He kept me looking respectable from the neck up.

When he first came to us Vic had gone through all the necessary security background checks and had an absolutely impeccable CV. He had cooperated fully with the constant monitoring required of intelligence personnel, and he was deemed eminently trustworthy. I found him comfortable to be with, easygoing, and a good listener. For some reason, I felt I could open up with him, and often did. He was, I felt instinctively, a man who would keep perfect confidentiality— a trait of his, admittedly, that had about it something of a steely Sicilian flavor, like something from the movies. When he talked, it was frequently about Italian wines and cooking, his love of Italy, which he said he visited annually, and various sports, particularly his favorite Italian football teams. He was not married and we never discussed his private life. He carried a rosary in the breast pocket of his immaculately white barber's shirt, which I couldn't help but notice on occasion, but we never spoke of religion.

He would come on Thursdays, precisely at ten in the morning, unless the schedule had to be altered, as frequently it did. But ten on Thursdays was usual, and—as I knew from my scrupulous secretary—no such alteration to the customary schedule had been made for that particular week when my abduction took place. In other words, I had expected him to come the Thursday of that week and not on the day and hour he actually did appear.

He showed up, in fact, on a Sunday evening. I was alone in my penthouse on the top floor of the SNARC Building, having lived there since my divorce, which had followed right on the heels of my second term as President of the United States. (Catherine, to her credit, had been considerate enough to wait until after I had left office before she left me.) Security personnel were, as usual, posted that night on the floors below and outside the entrance to the suite, and also above on the rooftop and in the darkened offices directly opposite across the street.

The multicolored lights of Manhattan, decked out in its "happy holidays" array, seemed only barely to glimmer through a murky vapor that had been sweeping over the city throughout the afternoon. A wind had begun to blow in from the ocean around four o'clock, softly and mournfully at first, then growing in intensity, in irregular and unexpected gusts so strong that their force rattled the fortified plated windows at times. This had been going on for hours by the time night fell. Looking out through the windows into the darkness, I could see ice crystals catch the light of my indoor lamps and flash like sparks. The night and the weather combined to seem (to me, at any rate) like a single great living creature on that particular evening, swirling about the skyscrapers in serpentine fashion, almost as if they possessed an impenetrable determination of their own.

Gloomy thoughts had been troubling my mind throughout the day and were still working on me that evening. As I stood now and looked out into that ominous turbulence, my mind and the outside environment seemed to be in sinister synchronicity. The lights inside my apartment were dimly lit, because I craved as much privacy as I could contrive for myself, and low lights contributed to that sense of seclusion. I had put up a small Christmas tree in the living room, my single gesture to honor the season, but its softly blinking colored lights contributed little brightness to the room. Somewhere out there in the murk those unseen security men were watching, always watching, poised and vigilant. No one, from above or below me, could ever get past them to get to me—of that I was certain. And that thought provided me with a modicum of comfort. But, at the same time, my feelings of security notwithstanding, I knew that they were watching *me*, and that awareness heightened my secret desire for a never-to-be-realized solitude.

I had been divorced for nearly two years at this time. So, when I was at home, I was "alone" (a man observed around the clock can never really be considered alone), and I had become—if not entirely used to my own somber company— at least not desperately lonely either. My sleep had been plagued by odd and worrisome dreams lately, and, being alone, these nightmares had a tendency to set the tone for my waking moods as well. And on this most evocative evening, with its dirty weather, the nightmare of the previous night— the one I've described already—haunted and oppressed my thoughts. I stood brooding on it while staring out at the curling and uncurling windy morass beyond the windowpanes.

I recall how preoccupied I was with it when, turning from the window and the blue sparks and the squall outside and the invisible presence of those security men across the way, and looking back into the dimly lit living room, I was startled to see the figure of a tall man wearing a long black coat and black fedora standing silently about ten feet from where I stood, silhouetted by the glow of the floor-lamp behind him.

Caught by surprise and a nearly heart-stopping pang of fear—for, how on earth had he gotten past the security personnel and into my apartment?—I cried out, quickly reaching for a heavy ashtray that lay on a coffee table near to hand, scattering cigarette butts and ashes all over the rug.

I brandished the object threateningly, and just as quickly realized I was looking into the eyes of my barber, Vic.

III

I LET out a stream of invective, mostly in relief, but my nerves felt shot for the next few moments while I got my breath and composure back. "Christ, Vic," I finally gasped, "What the hell are *you* doing here?"

Vic stepped forward and, taking the ashtray from my unsteady fingers, set it back on the coffee table.

"Thank you," he said, as if I had been intending to hand it over to him all along rather than to brain him with it. He casually produced from his coat a pack of cigarettes, tapped one out, put it in his mouth, and then offered me the pack inquiringly. I motioned I didn't want a smoke, and he casually lit up and said, "Sorry. I didn't mean to startle you, Mr. President."

Vic had been calling me "Mr. President" ever since I had been elected to my first term.

"What are you doing here?" I repeated, with restored composure now. "How did you get in without security stopping you?"

Vic motioned to the armchair that stood just to my right. "You'd better sit down and allow me to explain," he replied, and, without asking me if it was okay, he took a seat directly opposite mine, flicking the ash from his cigarette into the ashtray as he did so. His long coat, I saw, was unbuttoned and just then, as he was seated, it fell open, and I saw to my surprise that he was wearing a black cassock underneath it, as if he were a priest. I sat down in the armchair.

"Are you on your way to a costume party or something?" I asked him, pointing to the cassock. I didn't wait for an answer, but went on: "Never mind. Tell me what's going on. Who let you in here and why?"

"I won't beat around the bush," he answered calmly. "I'm here to pick you up and see to it that you meet with somebody very important before you go on to Oslo. I got past the security men outside because, to tell you straight out, I'm in charge of all your security personnel and have been, without you knowing it, ever since we met. Sorry if that sounds devious to you. I assure you, it's a security measure we employed for your safety. The time has come, however, to drop the pretense."

To say that I was confused by his words would be an understatement. I tried not to let it show that I was astonished, but I'm sure it was obvious to him. All I could manage to say was, "I'll take that cigarette." He tossed me the pack and I tossed it back after extracting one. He tossed me the matches and an instant later I was filling my lungs with smoke.

"There's a lot of things you don't know," he said. "That's going to change now, and that's one of the reasons I'm here. There's somebody you haven't met, but who's been waiting a very long time to fill you in with vital information—information about yourself, I should add—not only for your sake, but for everybody's sake. It's sensitive stuff, and you'll be in a better position to understand as soon as you've heard it out. It's my job to get you where you need to be to hear it."

"Can't you just tell me what this information is?" I said irritably, trying to take control of the situation. I wasn't used to being dictated to, not after decades of being in seeming charge, and the dawning recognition that I was certainly not in charge now, and maybe that I really hadn't been even before now, was disconcerting.

"I'm not the right person to fill you in," said Vic. "I'm just the messenger. The man I'm taking you to see is the man with the message. And, no," he added, seeing I was about to object, "it can't be put off. I know it'll sound ridiculous to you right now, under the circumstances, but the future of the world is at stake." And, with that, he stubbed out his cigarette in the ashtray hard and with a stiff twist of his fingers.

That my barber had been the true, anonymous organizer of my security forces for years had been an unexpected revelation, to say the least, but this additional disclosure—that there were secrets of which I had been kept in ignorance—was even more unsettling. A person in my position is expected to know what's going on, and this should certainly be the case in matters directly pertaining to himself and to his official role. For someone who had possessed, until recently, the nuclear football and its codes, it was difficult for me to realize that not only had I not known the identity of my own chief security officer, but that *someone else* possessed some sort of high priority intelligence of which I had until now, it seemed, been purposely kept in ignorance. I had, after all, built up the very corporation—SNARC—that had created an intelligence network capable of monitoring communications ceaselessly for use by authorized federal and international agencies. No one anywhere could get online or on any device without being instantly "observed" at Fort Meade, Langley, London, Paris, Tel Aviv, and elsewhere, thanks to the technologies devised at SNARC. Everyone's biography, work dossier, traffic violations, credit reports, email exchanges, phone records, etc., were all there, instantly accessible. And when I say "everyone," I mean *every single human being* on the planet who isn't a hermit isolated from society (and even then we could, if necessary, track down such a hypothetical hermit quickly enough). SNARC provided all the necessary keys to full personal accessibility globally, mainly for the sake of anti-terrorism intelligence. My company, in other words, had done much good, or so I believed. And I think we can legitimately say that terrorism as a tool has become less effective over the years—a scattered, hit-or-miss, "back alley" phenomenon with very small consequences, thanks to our efforts. Once implemented,

SNARC technology swiftly infiltrated, confused, and ultimately decimated various terrorist groups worldwide. And what wasn't accomplished by SNARC in the area of intelligence gathering was accomplished by SNARC in the area of superior weapons technology. We helped to kill a lot of "bad guys" (if you will pardon the expression) with SNARC tech. But, at any rate, it was intelligence technology especially that had originally been my own special field, and now I was finding out that there were secrets being kept even from me. This was a strange realization for me—in fact, it was a blow to my sense of competence and pride.

I stubbed out my own cigarette in the ashtray. "All right. I'll play along," I said, trying to sound in control of the situation, though I knew now that I wasn't, and I knew that he knew that I wasn't. "Who's this person you think I need to talk to, Vic—at this hour, in this weather?"

"I can fill you in as we travel," he said. "We got to get going now. Already packed for your Europe trip?"

"Yes," I said, with a sigh. "But I'm not scheduled to leave till tomorrow evening."

"We go tonight, Mr. President," said Vic with calm authority. "You receive the Peace Prize a week from tomorrow in Oslo. But before you do that, we need to fly you over to Rome."

"Rome isn't on my itinerary," I countered, feeling as if we were somehow now engaged in a futile match of wits. "Is that where I'm supposed to meet this mysterious character?"

"Actually, he lives out in the countryside not far from Rome." Vic stood up and began to button up his coat over his priest's cassock. I stood up, too. There was no use fighting something that seemed inevitable now. After all, whom could I call on to rescue me from my own security force?

"Beautiful country there," Vic continued. "A forested region. Not the finest time of year to visit, but you'll find his house comfortable."

14

For a moment or two we were silent, he standing there over me, the wind moaning outside, and ice crystals pattering against the panes. Finally I said:

"Tonight, you say? Has this been arranged without my knowing?" I don't know what possessed me to ask such a stupid question. It could have only one obvious answer.

"There was no other way."

"And arranged by the person we're going to see?"

"Yes," said Vic. "He arranged the meeting, and it was planned a long time ago."

"How long ago?"

"Years, actually."

"*Years?*" I said. "How many years?"

Vic smiled at the question. It wasn't a pleasant smile, either. I thought it looked distinctly sardonic under the shadow of his fedora.

"You wouldn't believe it if I told you," he said. "It's been centuries."

I took this strange remark to imply "a long time" and dropped it.

"But," he said, "let's get going. I'm not pulling rank here. Not really. I wouldn't insist on this if it weren't vital, as I said—for you and for the world. You've got to trust me on that."

I tried one final pushback. "What if I really don't think I can manage it tonight?" I countered. "Can I just say no to this invitation?"

"I'm afraid you can't do that," he said softly, but there was determination in his voice. "This is one time when your security forces must insist that you do as they say. You've got to leave New York and go with them to Rome tonight. You have no choice. But I assure you," he added a little consolingly, "that this will be the first and last time in your life that we'll insist on anything against your will."

Two more men came into the apartment at that instant, and I knew that Vic meant to take me by force if necessity

15

demanded. The newcomers were armed and wore black SWAT-style uniforms and berets with SNARC displayed on them.

"Hoisted on my own petard," I thought.

"Don't worry about them," said Vic. "They're here for your protection. If you tell me where you've stashed your bags, one of these guys will go get them. I suggest you put on a warm coat. It's freezing out there and we need to go up on the roof."

I indicated that my luggage was in the bedroom. I went to the hall closet and took out a long tweed coat and a scarf and bundled up. A few moments later we came out on the roof of the apartment building in the darkness and icy night air. Above our heads a helicopter circled, bright blue, white, and red lights flashing.

"Are we really going to fly in these conditions?" I shouted to Vic over the noise of the helicopter.

"What conditions?" he shouted back. And I realized then that the wind had ceased raging and there was now only a steady wintry breeze. The churning murk that had twisted itself around the tall buildings of Manhattan had completely disappeared.

The helicopter descended, and in a matter of seconds I was ushered inside it, along with Vic and the two men in SWAT gear who were carrying my bags, and we were lifted up and over the city.

IV

THE helicopter ride from the top of the SNARC Building to JFK lasted only a matter of minutes. During the trip I was in something of a mental fog, trying with difficulty to get back some grasp on my bearings and failing. Events had suddenly swept me up without warning and I confess I was deeply unnerved by it. I had never before felt more helpless than I did on that helicopter ride. I was used to exercising power from the top of the pyramid, which is a position at once lonely, but never alone, and wherein one is unable to appeal to anyone above oneself. Who could I turn to now except the very ones who were making off with me? I had no choice but to trust them.

We put down at the airport, and I was hustled off the helicopter and hastily escorted across shining wet tarmac by half a dozen additional men, also equipped SWAT-style, who seemed to come from nowhere. I realized that they were transferring me to my own personal jet, which, it was evident, had been made ready, its engines already whining loudly. Up the steps of the boarding ramp I was trundled by my "official" retinue and, once we were all aboard, the plane's door was shut and sealed behind us.

The interior of the cabin, at least, was familiar to me and, to a degree, that small fact was a little consoling. It had been laid out for comfort and convenience, according to my specifications, like a small living room. The seats were roomy and there were tables within convenient reach, and there was also a small kitchenette and bar. I removed my coat and scarf and handed them to one of the men, who promptly carried them out of the cabin. I sank with an audible sigh into my usual seat, and—somewhat reassuringly—I found myself being proffered a double scotch by Vic from the bar. He was now attired in the black priest's cassock, which had mystified me when I first spotted it beneath his coat. I received the whiskey from his hand and took a long sip of it. Its heat, flavor, and aroma acted like a restorative on me.

"We'll be taking off in a few minutes," said Vic. "I'll pour you another scotch once we're aloft. I've got some dinner for you, too. Pasta alla Puttanesca. I made it myself. It seemed like the right thing to serve on a trip over to 'Mystery Babylon'"—he smiled at this—"and I have a really nice Montepulciano d'Abruzzo to go along with it." He took the seat opposite me.

I sipped the whiskey and studied with renewed curiosity the features of this former Navy Seal turned barber turned chief security man and now turned cleric.

"What's with the priest clothes?" I finally asked him.

"Well, to be blunt, it's no ruse. I *am* a priest," he answered. "In fact, in Rome I hold the position of cardinal. You can see that my cassock has red piping. I'm not a bishop, though," he hastened to add, as if the distinction should make a difference to me. "Most cardinals are bishops, but I'm an exception. I'm known in Rome as Cardinal Silvestro. You can still call me Vic, though. I should mention that the man I'm taking you to see is also a cardinal—among other things. He's many years my senior in that office. Centuries my senior, in fact." He smiled again with the sardonic smile I had seen earlier, and again I took this mention of "centuries" as a metaphor. As yet, I had no clue of his real meaning.

"So... You're... a priest and a cardinal... *and* the head of my security people...?" I said as I finished my whiskey. "That's a hell of a lot to get used to all of a sudden. This morning you were only my barber. And a good barber, too," I added, absurdly. I realized how silly it sounded and changed the direction of my comments. "Who is this man we're going to see? *Another* cardinal...? Why? I'm not even Catholic..."

"Ah, the plane is taxiing into position," observed Vic. Then, looking me directly in the eye, he said, "To answer your question, the man we're going to see in Rome is Cardinal Fieropasto. You've never heard of him, I know. But he's very powerful and very influential, and he's been a mover of events for a very long time behind the scenes. He is, in fact, something more than a mere cardinal."

"You're right—I've never heard of him," I said. "More than a cardinal? If he's more than a cardinal, shouldn't that make him the pope?"

"You might think so," Vic said. "But, no. I'm not sure how to put it to you—what he is, that is. You'll see for yourself before too long, and you'll see that he's a very private gentleman. And he *is* a gentleman, a member of the nobility, in fact. And also—and this will be important for you to grasp—he's really the single most powerful individual in the world. Truth be told"—and here he leaned forward and looked at me with an intensity that seemed to bore right through my eye sockets to the very back of my skull—"he has always been that. For *centuries*, in fact."

He emphasized the word "centuries." I don't know why, exactly, but I reacted to his remarks with annoyance. Maybe it was the shot of whiskey working on me, but I abruptly felt that I had had enough of all this, and I wanted clear-cut, no-nonsense answers.

"Are you pulling my leg, Vic?" I said heatedly. "Is all this some sort of elaborate joke? Something to do with the coming holidays, maybe? Because, if it's not, I'm not getting it—I'm not getting any of this. I'm getting kidnapped by my own security men and whisked off to go see some 'very important person' who's a goddamned cardinal in Rome...? When did we fall down the rabbit hole? I missed that part."

Vic remained deadpan at this outburst, his sharp gaze still

fixed on me. "You aren't being kidnapped. And, to be frank, you couldn't understand at this stage what this is all about or how important it is for you to meet with Cardinal Fieropasto. How could you? I can understand what you must be feeling right now. I really can, and I'll try to fill you in with some of what you want to know, but it's not going to be easy for you to swallow. In fact, nothing about this will be easy for you. Cardinal Fieropasto is the right one to give you the most important details. But none of this is a hoax or a joke. You wouldn't guess it, but it's the culmination of a lifetime— *your* lifetime—of hard work and planning. And the *planning* wasn't done by you, but rather done *on your behalf by someone else*. Your rise to power over the years hasn't been an accident. It certainly wasn't your own doing. Your rise to power was inevitable. It's been in the works for a long, long while, since before you were even born. You'd be right to see it as predestination—*your predestination*." He softened his gaze and tone and, smiling, said, "But right now we're predestined to go to Rome, and before that to eat a good meal."

The plane was now cleared to take off and soon we were in the air and over the Atlantic.

For some minutes neither of us said anything. The others onboard, having removed their SWAT gear, were now in plain priests' cassocks (no red piping like Vic's), and they were seated in various positions, reading or looking at laptops or phones. Vic got up after the plane had reached its cruising altitude and poured me another double scotch, which I began to sip almost in a trance.

Dinner was then served, and I found myself inordinately hungry and grateful for the meal. After the two whiskeys, half a bottle of good red wine, and a warm dish, I confess I was even beginning to relax. Odd, I thought, that I should be accepting all this with growing equanimity. But, too, I really had no choice except to give up and give in and see where it all would lead. I had Vic's assurances, not that they made much sense to me and didn't involve unsettling qualms on my part. I was on my own plane and accompanied by my own security men—even if they were now all attired as clerics. If Vic was telling me the truth, I reassured myself, I would soon enough get to the bottom of this and get some explanations. I just had to be patient. I knew that my position in the world was unusual, that, sometimes at any rate, dedicated security and intelligence forces had to take charge of situations and were not free to disclose the reasons behind their actions even to those they were dutifully serving. The price someone like me had to pay on rare occasions was to be resigned and to put trust in others' loyalty and expertise.

And, in addition, I was simply too exhausted to worry about it anymore. The alcohol had deepened my drowsiness, and in that state I sank into a deep sleep.

...I was standing at the edge of the sea. There was a long pier that stretched out into the placid, black waters, and overhead there were great swelling dark clouds. In the distance, on the edge of the horizon, just below the curtain of clouds, I could see brilliant red-gold light streaming out over the waters, tinting the billows gaudily. All at once, I heard a plopping sound coming from the pier, and looked to see a large coal-black dog that had leapt out of the water and was now resting there, dripping. I thought it was a seal at first, but, no, it was a dog—or a seadog, perhaps, because its back end was legless. It had a furry fish's tail instead. And then I heard more plopping sounds, and saw that numerous similar seadogs were emerging from the water and beginning to move steadily in my direction. Before I knew it, there were what seemed to be dozens of the creatures, and they began moaning and yelping at me.

"Someone should put them back in the ocean," I said to myself. "Otherwise they'll get wet."

The seadogs kept clawing and flopping closer to me, and I

21

thought it might be best if I were to turn and make a dash into the woods behind me. Somehow I knew that that was what I needed to do and that I had only recently emerged from those woods myself. I also began to sense that the seadogs were driving me there intentionally. They were pressing me off the strand and towards the trees. I also knew that these animals were clergymen. I knew this purely intuitively, mind you, since they outwardly looked only like black fish-tailed dogs to me. I turned about and saw a tree standing alone between the dark wood and me, and in the tree there was a snake. This snake was not like any snake I'd ever seen before. It had two arms with which it held tightly to the bole of the tree, and two small, bat-like wings on its narrow shoulders. The rest of its supple body coiled round and round the trunk right down to the grass beneath. It was looking steadily in my direction, unblinkingly. I could have sworn that its sallow reptilian face was a human one, but only just barely.

At the base of the tree, as well, looking forlorn and doleful, were two shaggy apes eating neatly peeled bananas. They were no recognizable species of ape, but looked like men wearing the sort of gorilla costumes one sees in very old movies. They were wearing large fig leaves over their genitalia, and one appeared to have pendulous breasts. They looked at me glumly and chewed on their bananas.

And now the furry fish-tailed seadog clergymen were steadily pressing upon me, and I was moving ever nearer towards that tree, the ape-creatures, and the man-faced snake.

All at once the snake spoke to me:

"Did you bring your toothbrush?"

"Hmm? What?" I emerged from my dream as if coming up from the bottom of a weedy pond. I hit the surface. I felt and heard the airplane and opened my bleary eyes to see Vic standing in front of me.

"I was setting out your toiletries in the restroom and didn't see a toothbrush."

22

V

AFTER groggily telling Vic where he might find supplies such as an extra toothbrush onboard, I asked him how long I had been asleep. He said I had been out for a few hours and that we would be landing in another hour or so. Then he brought me coffee and some rolls with butter and jam. While he busied himself in the kitchenette and the other men were either dozing or preoccupied as they had been earlier, I drank my coffee and looked around the cabin.

Mid-morning sunlight streamed through the airplane windows, and a single beam fell on a red leather portfolio case next to the seat that Vic had occupied. I assumed it was his. But it wasn't the portfolio case that arrested my surprised attention. Rather, it was what was emblazoned on it that made something inside me sharply tingle as if from an electric shock. I could clearly see that there was a coat-of-arms adorning it, about six inches by six inches. The case was only about three feet away and I could make out the imagery clearly.

On a plain shield of royal purple was depicted a tree. Entwined about the tree was a serpent with two human arms that gripped the trunk and whose narrow shoulders sported small batwings. Its tiny, ruby-eyed face, which was turned fully towards the viewer, looked almost human. At the base of the tree on either side stood two shaggy apes wearing fig leaves, one of them with breasts, and both depicted with peeled bananas in their hands. Above the shield there was a cardinal's red hat, its cords and tassels curling elaborately round the shield on either side. Beneath the shield was the name "Fieropasto." and beneath that, on the image of an open scroll, the words, in Greek script: *"HO OPHIS HO ARCHAIOS."*

It was the image I had seen in my dream. Perhaps, I thought, I had seen the coat-of-arms before I slept without it having fully registered and that my unconscious mind had conjured it up in my dream. But I was sure that that wasn't the case. I felt certain I had never seen this disturbing image of the tree, the snake, and the two ape-creatures before my dream. The coincidence of seeing the same bizarre assembly reproduced on the portfolio case shook me. At that moment Vic reappeared and took his seat.

"Tell me," I said as he seated himself, "just who this Cardinal Fieropasto is. Is that his coat-of-arms on the portfolio case beside you? I can make out the Greek enough to pronounce it, but what's the inscription say?"

"Ah, that," said Vic. "Yes, it's Cardinal Fieropasto's arms. The inscription is *'HO OPHIS HO ARCHAIOS'*—it means 'The Ancient Serpent.' If you're wondering what's inside the portfolio, it's my report on 'Operation Bandersnatch,' Cardinal Fieropasto is a stickler for bureaucratic procedure, and he likes hard copy rather than electronic stuff. He's old-fashioned."

"'Operation Bandersnatch'? What's that?"

"Well, you are, actually," said Vic. "This operation we're engaged in now—bringing you to the Cardinal."

I turned that over in my mind for a moment or two. "And the coat-of-arms...? That's a hell of a picture."

Vic nodded. "Sure, it's unusual. Cardinal Fieropasto designed it. He had it done up in the mid-nineteenth century, to tell you the truth..."

"The *truth*?" I responded, an openly skeptical smile creeping across my face. "Come on, now. What's the real story?"

"That is the real story. I told you you'd find some facts about the Cardinal hard to swallow."

"So... You're actually telling me, in other words, that he's over a hundred years old."

"Yes, Mr. President, that's exactly what I'm telling you. And he's even a great deal older than that."

"Okay. How old? Try me."

"Very."

"And you're serious."

"Yes. I shouldn't be saying any of this to you, probably, but you'll need to know it soon enough anyway, and you've already been brought this far. So, here goes. Cardinal Fieropasto is much, much older than the human race itself. No, please don't interrupt. Let me continue first. He's not, technically speaking, human at all, although he's flesh and blood and will remain so until his death."

I very nearly laughed out loud at this, but more out of befuddlement than amusement.

"So," I said, "he can die…?"

I saw that Vic appeared to be sincere, that he seemed to believe what he was telling me. Of course, I thought, there must be some reasonable explanation for this. Fieropasto was a person powerful enough, I had good reason now to accept, to commandeer my personal security forces behind the scenes and to engineer my abduction—something I wouldn't have thought achievable by anybody before now. But I couldn't believe that this powerful figure—whoever he might be—was in some sense superhuman and astoundingly ancient. Such absurd claims must be delusional, I thought to myself. And even highly intelligent and seemingly well-balanced persons, such as Vic, could irrationally be drawn to accept absurdities.

"Yes," said Vic. "He can die, and will die. That much is certain. He knows it and talks about it, and I think he even sometimes desires it." Vic leaned back in his seat, eyes half closed, as he said this.

"Okay, then," I said. "Let's say I accept what you're telling me—for the sake of argument, at least. So, who or what is he?"

"He's been described as 'going to and fro in the earth, and walking up and down on it.'"

I'm a pretty literate guy. "That's in the Bible," I said. "It's talking about Satan."

"Very good. You deserve a gold star. The book of Job, in fact."

I thought of the coat-of-arms and the motto in Greek— "The Ancient Serpent"—another biblical quote, a phrase from the book of Revelation. I thought of the snake coiled in the tree and the two apes at its foot and I felt a funny sensation in the pit of my stomach.

"Vic, are you telling me that this person—that this person believes that, in some way, he's linked to the devil or, maybe, *is* the devil? The devil in the Bible?"

"Don't judge him for that," replied Vic. "It's more complicated than that. Suspend your opinions until you meet him. Reality isn't always as black and white as we'd like it to be. Keep in mind that the Cardinal is also a distinguished member of the hierarchy of the Church, with a reputation for personal integrity. He's been one of the great architects of canon law, for instance. He's a highly esteemed gentleman who's held an honored position for ages."

"His coat-of-arms looks pretty sardonic to me. That weird symbolism," I said, pointing to it, "is damned unsettling."

"Ah," said Vic with arched eyebrows. "The story behind that is that it was originally just a bit of dark humor. Back when Darwin was making his big splash, another cardinal sketched that coat-of-arms on a napkin to amuse Cardinal Fieropasto at some banquet or other, since he didn't have a coat-of-arms at the time. Of course, like so many in the highest ranks of the hierarchy, he knew who Cardinal Fieropasto really was. But he couldn't help ribbing him on this occasion, so the story goes, and he drew this design. To the delight of the artist, Cardinal Fieropasto nearly fell off his chair laughing when he saw it—and Cardinal Fieropasto rarely laughs.

He liked the sketch so much he had it done up in real style, and now he uses it as his personal seal."

I was nonplussed. It was hard to know how to react to the revelation that apparently there was at the Vatican a highly respected Prince of the Church who passed himself off as Satan incarnate, and that this was a matter of ongoing acceptance, concealment, and even amusement. Vic's seemingly casual explanation of what looked to me like an insulting cartoon, not just acerbic and mocking, but suggestive of the most caustic appraisal of human worth, wasn't terribly reassuring either.

"You seem to take this rather unconcernedly," I said, "as if it's all somehow conventional. Is it—I mean, is it *conventional* in the circles you frequent?"

"There's no question that Cardinal Fieropasto has, let's call it, an astringent sense of humor," said Vic. "Not everyone appreciates it."

We sat silently for a few moments. Then Vic said, "There's a few things the Cardinal wants to say to you man-to-man, Mr. President. Still, to prime you for that, I'll tell you now that he sees you as uniquely positioned to do the world much good. He says he believes you alone can undo some harm he himself caused ages ago. He wants very much to confide in you what he's been unable to tell another living soul, not even his closest confidants, up to now."

"I'm not following you, Vic," I said. "This guy sounds mentally disturbed. I don't know what else to make of all this."

"Think for a moment," said Vic, ignoring the challenge of my comment. "Think. Think of the role you play in the world. You are in a position to assume unprecedented leadership in the world."

"And Fieropasto is... is... the devil..." I could barely bring myself to say it, so fabulously foolish it sounded.

"I know it's hard to swallow," said Vic, understandingly.

A light suddenly, rather sickeningly switched on in my

head. "He wants me," I said dryly, "to help him do something? He thinks he's the devil and he wants me to do something for him? You know, Vic, your position with me—not as my barber, but as whatever else you are—is at risk of being terminated as soon as this damn-fool adventure is over."

"Well," he retorted with a smile, "it's a very good thing, then, that I'll still have my night job as a cardinal."

"What does Fieropasto want from me, then?" I said.

"That, I think, is for him to explain to you personally." Vic replied. "But right now, please put on your seatbelt. We're about to land."

VI

THERE are a few methods that can be employed to help protect an important official's security, though briefly, in a public setting. One of these methods is simply to have an easily recognizable person dress in a fashion that isn't customary or associated with that person's known persona, careful to make sure that his or her features are obscured enough that facial recognition and retinal scanning devices aren't effective, and then to move rapidly through the public area with no visible security personnel around oneself at all—one's security personnel are, of course, on hand, but in plainclothes. Assuming that the person's presence is wholly unpublicized and unexpected, he or she usually can move virtually unseen through a crowd for a short time. Even if somebody might note the "resemblance" that the disguised person bears to his well-known public face, most people assume that, since so-and-so couldn't possibly be out in public like this or dressed like this, this doppelganger couldn't possibly be the genuine article. And most people in crowds are also less observant of others' features than one might suppose. You yourself may have rubbed shoulders with a famous celebrity or an important personage and not realized it. It was in this way I was moved through the airport in Rome.

I wore a priest's cassock and collar, as Vic and the security men did. We had old-fashioned black "fried egg" priest's hats on our heads and I was given dark glasses to wear as well, and we looked every inch like a pack of Iberian clergy on holiday or pilgrimage or business, making our way to the Vatican. Nobody so much as glanced at my features. From there we passed through various checkpoints, but with a word or two from Vic—Cardinal Silvestro, that is to say—we were always waved through.

From there we eventually made our exit to a waiting black stretch limousine outside. On each of its front doors and also reproduced on two small fluttering flags above the car's headlights, I saw displayed the Fieropasto coat-of-arms. A second car—a black Range Rover—was waiting directly behind the limousine. It, too, was adorned with the Cardinal's emblem, and seated within it were additional, grim-looking, square-jawed, uniformed security men wearing dark glasses. The security men who had accompanied me from New York now occupied the forward section of the stretch limousine, while the rear section, cut off and soundproofed for VIP use, had been reserved for Vic and me.

Before departing the plane we had eaten a large breakfast, an American style one of steak and eggs, and so I was feeling fortified with high protein and caffeine. I was as ready as I would ever be, I felt, for a meeting with the enigmatic cleric who claimed to be immensely old and—not to put too fine a point on it—his Satanic Majesty. If it was true that he made such outlandish claims, here at least was someone who possibly might outdo Aleister Crowley for diabolic audacity. I was, of course, not ready to believe these claims myself, but I could well believe that whatever else this individual might prove to be, given how he had apparently convinced others to credit his claims, he would clearly be extraordinary. And, besides, what if his age really was some sort of biological mystery, an exception to the rules of human longevity? Maybe he truly was vastly old. Simply because the mass of humanity didn't live for hundreds of years, did that make it a foregone conclusion that someone quite unique might not just conceivably prove immune to normal standards of aging? The oldest Greenland sharks are at least six hundred years old. If Greenland sharks can live so long, then why not a single, highly unusual *homo sapiens*? Perhaps his very length of life had made him and others believe that he didn't even belong to the same species?

My own life had been a long series of unprecedented occurrences, so—I told myself—why not this strange new turn of events? I was beginning to suspect that possibly the very nature of everything I thought I understood was about to be proved mistaken, that a seismic shift was about to take place in how I viewed everything. I confess I even wondered if, perhaps, I might find myself being personally favored for initiation into arcane knowledge—into some deep secret that, as so many illuminated minds have suspected, has lain beneath all our civilized institutions going right back to the ancient world? "Secret knowledge" had never before been something I thought much about (Freemason though I am). Groups and societies that claimed hidden knowledge I tended to dismiss as spurious, not serious. The fear of secret societies one found, say, in the Roman Catholic Church, seemed hysterical and overwrought to my mind. I knew first-hand, for instance, that the Freemasons today were about as conniving and dangerous as the Boy Scouts. Similarly, the historical Knights Templar had never really possessed any-thing earth-shattering in the way of "secrets," the Hellfire Club had been merely a bunch of aristocratic drunks with a propensity for orgies and playing at faux Satanism, the Illu-minati had mostly been fantasy and posturing, and so on; and all the other far-fetched secret societies and occult broth-erhoods beloved of conspiracy theorists and religious fanat-ics down the years had never really posed threats to anyone except those stupid enough to take the nonsense seriously. If one wanted to locate a true cabal with secret knowledge and conspiratorial influence, one had only to consider the CIA or FBI—with whom I've had a long, sometimes difficult, but usually amicable association. After all, as I said earlier, I had been someone "in the know," and these were things I knew and had used to my own advantage.

31

But, even so, there has always been reason to think that even those "in the know" couldn't know everything; that the average lifespan of a single man or the length of time given to each generation would not be sufficient to find out an underlying "conspiracy" if one exists, especially if it were an ongoing unfolding mega-narrative that ties all of history together, gathering up all the threads from the Pharaohs to India to China to Mesopotamia to Alexander to the Romans to Christendom to the founding of the United States and beyond. And somehow it has always seemed to come back to Rome, as to a center, and therefore to the Roman Catholic Church, that repository and continuation of ancient Western civilization. In the popular imagination this has also been the supposition, to judge from any number of novels and films (most of them, of course, ridiculous). I was finding out, perhaps, that there might just be more truth to this perennial suspicion than I would have believed. Something had been undeniably brewing and stewing in Rome and within the Vatican for centuries, and perhaps there really were mysteries there that were about to be revealed to me.

Perhaps Cardinal Fieropasto was not at all crazy, despite all the rubbish about his being the devil. Perhaps this mysterious dignitary sincerely wished to disclose a confidence that might make sense of so many other things that needed to be made sense of. I confess that I experienced a momentary thrill at this new, startling, but enticing idea, one that I can't describe adequately and which would normally have been so uncharacteristic of me—as if something of immense significance, a mystery concealed for ages, was about to be laid open, and that I was now, at this hour, chosen to be its recipient. In other words, I was beginning to suspend my disbelief a little.

VII

IT was a long and unremarkable drive from the airport out into the countryside, and eventually off the beaten path altogether. The time of year was late autumn turning to winter, and the landscape reflected it. Shades of brown interspersed with the dark green of pine and mosses, skies like sheet metal, a smattering of rain, the skeletons of deciduous trees, and the few remaining leaves that clung stubbornly to them mostly the color of rust.

No one spoke during the journey, which lasted the better part of two hours. I merely looked out the window at the passing landscape, lost in thought. I wanted to phone Catherine, at least, and let her know where I was. Our relations were still cordial enough. But I was informed that my phone had been deactivated "for security reasons." At some point during the ride, I realized we were in a region that was increasingly wooded, and soon we were plunged into a thick forest of evergreens. The road here was unpaved and rough going, and the frequent jolts were buffeting. But, at last, underneath a canopy of pines whose limbs were so densely tangled that the cloudy sky above was obscured, I made out a gray wall of stone, and a portal of iron before us. Outside the gate stood a wooden, peak-roofed sentry booth, painted a drab olive-green. Above the iron gate, carved into the stone façade, was once again the Fieropasto coat-of-arms, this time colorless, weatherworn, obviously old, and festooned with leafless vines. A bird's nest was just visible atop the head of the ape with the breasts, giving her the appearance of wearing a seedy, battered cap.

As we came up alongside the sentry booth, inside I could

see a wizened little man in a yellow jacket and wearing a yellow sports cap. Without saying a word, he pulled a switch of some sort just out of my range of vision, and the gate swung open creakily and slowly. Our two vehicles passed through.

We continued down the path, overshadowed by the great pines, past old granite fountains, dry and lifeless and ivy- or moss-covered, past statues of marble, some leaning backwards or forwards or sideways and some broken, armless, or headless, or off their pedestals and strewn about like the corpses after a battle, all of them gods and goddesses and heroes of the classical pantheon. We drove on for what seemed a stretch of five kilometers or so, and then, before us, almost as if built into and emerging out of the wood itself, an immense gray stone structure, the size and shape of which could only be guessed, so surrounded and nearly encased in the tree limbs was it.

The style of its architecture I could only conjecture, but what little I could see of it looked like Italian Gothic. That it rambled on, obscured by the boughs of the trees, I could observe, but its height was impossible to tell. The facade appeared, in fact, to be a cliff-side and a castle simultaneously, a mountain that also happened to be a fortress, its true dimensions camouflaged by evergreens. It was before this unlikely forest bastion that our vehicles came to a stop, and we got out and made our way to two enormous doors, made of what looked to be thick oak, each standing about fifteen feet in height. Once more, above the doorway and carved into a single large block of stone, was the ubiquitous Fieropastian coat-of-arms.

Vic looked quite somber as he led the way. "It'll be fine," he said to reassure me, but I noticed that he appeared a little wary himself now. Up to this point his demeanor had been one of confidence and authority, but now I discerned in his movements the gait of someone who knows he is approaching a seat of power. Nothing fawning, mind you, just a grave demeanor and a bearing of formal dignity.

"This was once the site of an Etruscan town," he remarked. "These hills—in fact, the very ground beneath our feet—are festooned with caves the Etruscans dug out. There's a collection of their artifacts here—armor, implements of all sorts, pottery, religious objects, and so on. Remarkably ancient paraphernalia. Fieropasto has extended the underground system of caves over the years, as you might just see for yourself."

As we drew near, I looked off to one side of the great double doors and saw, seated on a stoop beside a large tree trunk, a short, frog-faced, bald man, rather epicene in his appearance. He was dressed in bright yellow, and had enormous boots on. On his lap, sitting upright, was a small dachshund. The man was eating green gelato from a paper cup with a plastic spoon, and after each one of his own mouthfuls he gave the dog one to lick from the same spoon. He looked up at us, and in very good English said, "You know, their mouths are cleaner than ours."

Some remarks have no adequate response. The little man seemed almost agitated as he said it, as if he expected an argument from us, or thought that we—and I in particular, for some reason—disapproved of his dining arrangements with the dachshund. I said something innocuous, but the frog-faced man merely looked at me with evident displeasure as he thrust another spoonful of gelato into his mouth, and then held out another to the eager little dog. The dog lunged suddenly for the spoon and knocked it, gelato and all, onto the man's yellow trousers.

"No, Cerberus!" said the man to the dog, smacking the tip of his nose with the spoon. "Bad boy." He pulled out a red handkerchief and dabbed at the gelato on his pants, then picked up the spoon and resumed sharing his treat with the quivering little beast.

"Don't mind Mr. Charlie," whispered Vic in my ear. "He's one of the residents here."

"Residents?" I whispered back.

"Yes. The Cardinal has the reputation of possessing a soft spot for such unfortunates."

"Does he indeed?" I said, not really sure what kind of "unfortunates" we were talking about.

"You can judge for yourself when you meet him," replied Vic. "We can talk about it later."

Vic went up to the doors now, grasped one of the two large cast-iron rings that served as knockers, and pounded three times heavily. One of the doors opened inward, and there stood an elderly gentleman, tall and gaunt with long gray hair that fell to his shoulders, reminding me of photographs of Franz Liszt, dressed in a rather shabby and spotted clerical cassock. He had a pinched, sharp face and his lips were pursed as if he had sucked lemons so many times that his mouth had shriveled into a permanent pucker.

"Welcome back, your Eminence," he said to Vic in an Oxbridge accent. "And this must be the honorable Mr. President. Welcome." He took my hand with his own wrinkled, prominently veined, parchment-colored one and shook it vigorously. "Indeed," he said, "welcome ninety times nine."

"Mr. President, this is Father Snithering, Cardinal Fieropasto's personal secretary," said Vic. "He'll take you to your room and give you some orientation later. You'll need it—this is a very large place."

Which, indeed, it was. As my eyes adjusted to the dark interior, I saw that I was standing in what looked almost like a great stone amphitheater, with a ceiling so high above me that it was lost in the shadows. What lighting there was came from a number of scattered, softly glowing floor lamps. There was not a window in sight. Clustered here and there in this vast open space were leather sofas and armchairs, as in an old-fashioned British men's club. Around me, and ascending upwards for what looked like at least nine stories, were balconies with rows of doors on each floor, and above each door there was a lamp, as in an apartment building or a grand hotel plaza. These floors seemed to spiral upwards; and I could see two large staircases to my extreme right and left, and next to each stairway the polished bronze sliding doors of an elevator. It looked at once like a huge hotel lobby, a small city, and a medieval castle.

But what struck me even more was the population that milled about the precincts: dozens of shuffling men, some young and some old, attired in the same striking yellow I had seen on Mr. Charlie outside, among whom a number of priests and (as I was to learn) religious brothers were moving. Apparently, these acted as attendants. There were also a few elderly nuns about—evidently nurses, judging from their stethoscopes and aprons, which they wore in addition to their habits—who were evidently quite solicitous of their yellow-clad charges.

Father Snithering noticed how I looked about, and said, "Perhaps Cardinal Silvestro didn't mention that this is a sort of asylum—a sort of refuge—which Cardinal Fieropasto founded a long time ago for such patients as these."

"No," I said, casting a glance at Vic. "He didn't tell me anything about this place."

"I thought it was the sort of thing you should see for yourself first," said Vic.

"I see. Well. May I take you to your room first?" asked Father Snithering. "You may like to freshen up or rest a bit, before I show you around and introduce you to your host."

I glanced at Vic, who only looked at me and nodded.

"Yes," I said. "That will be fine."

"Follow me, then," said Father Snithering and gestured toward the elevator doors off to our left.

VIII

THE three of us walked across the indoor amphitheater, past huddled clumps of men in yellow and their attendants, and entered the elevator. Behind us followed one of the security men carrying my luggage. Father Snithering pushed the button marked "10" and the car ascended.

"You will, of course, be given the special guest suite, which I hope you will find to your liking," he said.

The elevator doors slid open and we stepped out into a broad hallway. Father Snithering led the way down the hall about six yards until we came to a polished oak door, which he unlocked and then motioned for me to go in ahead of him. The security man followed us in, set down my luggage, and disappeared. The three of us—Father Snithering, Vic, and I— now stood in a luxuriously furnished suite. Here there was light streaming in through two large French windows in the main sitting room. There was, in addition to the sitting room, a bathroom and bedroom, and each room—including the bathroom—was equipped with a fireplace. The bed was huge, canopied, and inviting, and, as I had a headache coming on, it seemed to beckon to me. All I wanted to do was collapse on it.

"Cardinal Silvestro's rooms are next to yours," said Father Snithering. "You look as if perhaps you would like to rest now. I'll leave you here and come back in a little while. In an hour, say?"

I thanked him and he left.

Vic stood there for a moment and then said, "I'm going to leave, as well. I'll see you again when Snithering shows up."

"What is this place, Vic?" I asked, ignoring his words. "What sort of patients are these—what sort of asylum?"

"It's not exactly a mental institution, if that worries you."

"No, that doesn't worry me," I countered. "I just want to know what sort of place you brought me to."

"These men have special problems, requiring a special type of charity," said Vic. "I'll explain later on—or perhaps Snithering or the Cardinal will."

"The Cardinal who believes he's Satan. Very reassuring."

"Of course," said Vic, "we don't call him that here. 'Satan' isn't who he is now. It's who he was a long time ago. The centuries have altered him. You're not the adolescent you once were, are you? Well, neither is he. Don't expect to see much of the fallen angel in him. Not that there was ever a lot of that to start with. Anyway, you'll be meeting him soon and you'll understand what I'm talking about."

"Well, it's just that I thought the devil was—you know—a 'spiritual' being. A fallen angel, not a man and not someone who changes, not able to repent, condemned forever…"

"We're not literalists here," answered Vic. "Perhaps Brother Antoine comes close. He's Father Snithering's personal assistant, a Dominican brother. He's young, old-fashioned, a traditionalist. At any rate, what you're calling 'Satan' is always out there, lurking around 'like a lion greedy for its prey.' Psychologically speaking, you could say there's untamed evil inside everybody, even if it's only potential evil. That's the 'Satan' we should be really afraid of. As for a personal 'devil'… well, as I told you, he's changed."

"So the Church has lied about the devil for centuries."

"The Church has kept her secrets; and once the hierarchy realized who this person was who walked among them with such nobility, and saw how ably and well he performed his duties, and how much was owed him, and how respectful he had become—well, they felt they had to shield one of their own."

Vic turned towards the door. "Get some rest now. It's all going to get clearer to you from here on out. When you leave, you won't be the same man you were when you came in. The things you'll learn here will change you, but you'll also understand why it was crucial to bring you here. I can't tell you what Cardinal Fieropasto wants to say to you himself. But, remember this: you can trust me. I'm your man whenever you need me."

"I certainly hope so, Vic," I said. "You know I'm not a man who likes being jerked around. You got me here and I haven't put up much of a fuss about it because we go back a few years and I've always liked you. But this had better resolve itself, or else I'll have no choice but to…"

But I didn't have any idea now how I might intimidate him, so I just let my unfinished sentence hang in the air.

"Like I said, you can trust me," he said, unmoved by my bluster. And with that he left.

With head aching, I made my way to the large bed, stretched out on it with a groan, and almost instantly fell into a deep sleep.

IX

I AWOKE at the sound of rapping outside the door of my suite. Father Snithering was in the hallway, with Vic beside him, and I joined them. We proceeded down the hall, Father Snithering taking the lead.

"I cannot possibly show you the entire complex in one go," said Snithering as the elevator made its descent. "It's much too large for that. But I can at least give you some idea of what it comprises."

The doors of the elevator slid open and we stepped out into the amphitheater that had met my eyes when I first stepped into the edifice.

"This is what we call our Grand Hall," said Snithering. "It's the oldest part of the building. The original foundations were laid in the sixth century, modified significantly in the tenth, and so on many times until the present day. The elevators were finally installed, after some discussion, in 1963. The most recent additions to the complex—an all new computerized heating system, for instance—were made only last year."

There was still the bustle of persons moving about in the large central area, and I began to note certain oddities in the patients. They were, as I've indicated, all males. One fat old man leered at the standing potted plant he sat beside, whispering what I guessed were obscene intentions to it and gesturing emphatically to his crotch. At intervals he emitted loud snorts. Standing out in the open were two younger men who talked and gesticulated energetically, but with motions so exaggerated that they looked as if they were acting out a ridiculous pantomime. Just off to my right a group of five, one unabashedly picking his nose with his thumb and another farting so audibly I could hear it from some feet away, shouted angrily at one another. And in another spot out in the open, a steel-haired sister was taking the blood pressure of a man in a wheelchair, as all the while he looked about him jerkily and made grimaces. Similarly unhappy scenes were being played out in all directions.

Snithering noted my roving eyes and uneasiness. "It's their recreation hour," he said, by way of explanation.

Some priests and brothers were mingling with the patients, and I saw one earnestly hearing the confession of one aged fellow less than twenty feet away, their two armchairs pulled up close together and the priest wearing a violet stole. I could see, despite all the care they were receiving, that there was a perceptible vacuity in the eyes of all these men in yellow. There was a blankness in every face, as if everything in this place was really devoid of all hope or the possibility of any genuine cure, and that it no longer mattered at all to any of them, if it ever had, anyway. Even when their gestures were animated, there was nothing but deadness in their eyes. They looked haunted or possessed. I had seen the same expression, when I first arrived, on the face of Mr. Charlie, the frog-faced man, even as he had exhibited displeasure at my presence, and here it was again and again around me on every side.

"Tell me about the patients," I said to my guides.

Father Snithering turned his sharp face towards me, his petrified pout looking rather sinister to me at that instant, and said, "What do you want to know about the patients?"

"What is it exactly they suffer from?" I asked. "Vic—Cardinal Silvestro—told me they weren't mentally ill, but many of them look that way to me."

"Madness? No. But, yes, each suffers a malady of soul," replied Snithering in a tone that was meant, I felt, to come across as indicative of beneficence. "It's a charity that very few others would consider taking on, but it's our longstanding mission in this home. All these men have suffered terribly, and for them Cardinal Fieropasto has provided special treatment."

"I don't quite understand," I said.

"It's simple enough," said Vic. "Think of one class of people almost nobody except an especially caring person would be concerned about, not to mention have around in close proximity. A class of people despised even by other criminals..."

"Criminals?"

"Yes," said Vic.

I thought for a moment, and then said hesitantly: "Criminals—criminals detested by *other* criminals. All I can think of are those who've abused children." I felt uncomfortable even saying it.

"And who will care for such persons?" asked Father Snithering. "It takes an uncommon man to think of the lowest of the low in society's eyes, and to see to it that even they have a place to live out their lives while people everywhere else shun them."

The vacuity in the eyes of these men now seemed more troubling to me than before. I saw no sign of consolation in their eyes, no sign of life or warmth. I recalled the words of Mr. Charlie to the small dog earlier out on the doorstep—"Bad boy!"—and they now rang in my ears in a newly unsettling way. I felt a wave of biliousness rise up in me, and my headache—which hadn't subsided during my nap—began to throb with renewed intensity. All I wanted to do was get away from all these repellent dead-eyed men in their yellow costumes.

"This place has been a shelter for such unfortunates since the late-twelfth century," continued Father Snithering in tour-guide mode. "Founded by the Cardinal in 1183."

"I feel very little sympathy for abusers of children," I said honestly and with growing agitation. "Even Jesus had hard words about them—something about drowning with millstones." I was feeling revulsion and indignation now, exacerbated by my aching head.

"I think," said Father Snithering dulcetly, "that that only underscores the compassion of Cardinal Fieropasto. He is a man who offers sympathy even to those fit, at best, for a heavy sentence. That surely counts as remarkable charity on his part."

"More charitable maybe than Christ...?"

"I'm sure our Lord was not saying that such men as these should suffer if instead forgiveness might be shown them." Snithering waved his hand benignly towards the patients. "Look at them. They're miserable. They can't act out their appetites anymore. They're away from temptation. Children are kept well away from them. In most cases, their transgressions were committed years ago. Could you, in all honesty, throw the first stone at any one of them? Believe me, I understand your sentiments. Yours is the most common reaction, in fact. But that's precisely why they're here and not outside, on the street and in society. Here they find a refuge."

I said nothing in response. There was no point in registering any further disgust.

So, we moved on. I was conducted through corridors, up back staircases, through cloisters, through indoor gardens, bathing areas, refectories, and kitchens. I was shown meeting rooms, medical facilities, a dentist's office, a place for a barber to groom the residents ("Nicest barbershop I've seen anywhere," remarked Vic), and areas set aside for recreation and merely for lounging about. There was a tennis court, a place for volleyball, shuffleboard, chess sets, and other sports and gaming resources. The complex was mind-bogglingly huge and rambling, and by the time I was brought back to my own suite of rooms I wasn't any better oriented that I had been at the beginning of the tour. When I did return to my rooms, I saw that a hot meal had been laid out for me moments before in the main sitting room in my absence.

"At eight o'clock, following Compline, the Cardinal will meet with you," Father Snithering said. "In the meantime, please relax and enjoy your meal." He then bowed his head courteously and exited the suite.

I turned to face Vic, who lingered at the entrance for a moment. "Will you be there when I meet the Cardinal?" I asked.

"No, but it should go fine," replied Vic. "I'll say goodnight to you now. I'm sure you'll find the Cardinal a stimulating conversationalist." And with those words, Vic left, shutting the door behind him as he went.

With both men now gone, I sat down to roast duck, greens, and potatoes. Eight o'clock was two hours away, and I thought I would take something for my pounding headache and lie down to rest before the fateful meeting that lay in store for me.

X

I MET him before ever laying eyes on him. He came to me in a dream.

In my dream I was lying on the bed precisely as I was in reality, and he was standing at its foot. He was a small, somewhat birdlike man, dressed in a black cassock with red piping such as Vic had worn, with a scarlet sash around his middle. His complexion was sallow, and he had pale gray eyes that shone dully with yellowish tints. Thin strands of gray hair were slicked back against his skull, and on his head he wore a scarlet zucchetto. He was certainly old, but he didn't look sickly in any way. The face had no wrinkles, oddly enough, even though he appeared aged otherwise; it had a reptilian quality, reminding me of the snake's features on the ubiquitous coat-of-arms. His form was small, with an almost feminine delicacy. His voice, when he spoke, was high-pitched and nasal, with an acerbic edge—the sort of voice that lends itself to ironic asides, cutting and sneering remarks, and, in another modulation, whining self-pity. But what he now said to me, as I stared back at him as he stood there and stared at me, belied these unpleasant adjectives. Despite the annoying tone of his voice, his words were all sincerity and graciousness.

"I am Cardinal Fieropasto," he said. "I welcome you to my home. I have longed for our meeting since the day you were conceived. I have come to you first in this unusual way to reveal to you that I am indeed all that you've been told concerning me—although I am, of course, also under no illusion that this intrusive demonstration will convince you quite yet. It can only serve as a small piece of evidence for the time being. But you see how easily I can slip into your mind. Now,

46

I want to be entirely honest and open with you, my son, and the sooner you know both my capabilities and my wishes for you, which are entirely in your best interests, the better. I have much to say to you, and the time is short."

He reached up to his forehead with the index finger and thumb of his right hand and took from it, from between his eyes, as if out of his own skull, a tiny bright blue orb of light. He put the glowing, marble-sized orb into the palm of his other hand, raised it before his pale lips, and then blew it sharply in my direction. The small light came towards me so rapidly that I had no time even to blink. There was a flash in my head, as if the light had exploded behind my eyes, and instantly I awoke.

XI

FROM where I lay on the bed I could see over my feet and through the open bedroom door that the lights in the sitting room were on. I knew I had turned them off before my nap. Then, from that room, I heard a familiar voice—*his voice*, the voice I had just heard in my dream—and it said:

"Come in! Come in, and know me better, man."

Something stirred in my memory at those words. I slipped out of the bed, put on my shoes, tucked my shirt into my pants (I had taken off the cassock shortly after my arrival), and walked out into the other room.

Sitting in one of the two dark green leather armchairs there, a fire blazing in the hearth nearby, was the very man I had met only moments before in my dream, still dressed in his cardinal's cassock and zucchetto. I suddenly recalled what the scene reminded me of—it was Scrooge waking up to find the Ghost of Christmas Present in his apartments. In my case, though, the visitor possessed markedly less cheer.

"Now that you are awake," he said, rising from the chair with his pale hand extended, "allow me to greet you properly." I shook his hand. It was clammy and bony, almost amphibian to the touch. He motioned to the other armchair, which was nearer the fireplace. "Welcome again to my home. Ninety times nine welcome, as we say around here. I do apologize," he added, putting a finger beside his nose, "for invading your sleep just now, but I thought it might be an effective way to introduce myself. As a rule, I disdain theatrics. I dislike all forms of sensationalism, really. Much like yourself, I believe."

By now I had become so used to unusual things happening

that I took this whole unlikely scene in stride. It seemed almost normal to me now that this man should occupy both my dream life and waking life. Beside his chair on a three-legged table were a tall dark blue bottle and two glasses. He poured a dark amber liquid into the glasses from the bottle and held out one of them for me to receive.

"You are, I trust, rested—no trace of jetlag?" he inquired casually.

"None," I replied as I reached over and took the glass from his hand.

"And your head—no more headache?"

I had to admit to myself that I was feeling quite refreshed. "My headache is gone," I said, and took a sip of what was a very pleasant cream sherry. "I guess you had something to do with that? Was it... some sort of *magic*?" I felt ridiculous posing the question in that manner.

Fieropasto arched his wispy gray eyebrows at that. "Magic? No, not in the least," he said. "Well, on second thought, I suppose such exhibitions of pure science might seem like magic at times. But 'magic' per se... no. Everything I do is done through technology; and technology is, I suppose you might say, natural law stripped of nature itself and—as an abstraction—able to be distilled into manipulable, workable law. I thought you would need your wits about you, so I used a bit of technology of my own devising, a 'psychological tool' you could call it, and—*voila!*—here you sit, right as rain."

He took a mouthful of the sherry and I did, too. For some moments we sat before the fire like two old men who had nothing much to do and sipped our drinks. Then he said softly in his nasal tones, "The circumstances surrounding your visit here have undoubtedly been very trying for you, and I will do my utmost to see that you are relaxed during your stay with us. But, since our time together on this occasion must be short, you will need to be attentive as well. I have some very important things to say to you, and it will require all your concentration to take them in as you should."

"I don't know what to say to you, Cardinal," I replied. "Is that the correct protocol, calling you 'Cardinal'?"

"Call me 'Cardinal,' if you wish. 'Your Excellency' strikes me as much too grand. Or call me 'Father,' if you prefer. Perhaps I should call you 'Mr. President,' as Cardinal Silvestro does. I have been in the habit for ages of calling people 'my son' or 'my daughter,' so forgive me if I should slip into that style of address." He smiled again, and I noticed that when he smiled his mouth formed a small, rather unsettling "v."

"Well, then, I don't know what to say to you, Cardinal," I went on. "Clearly, you already own my security men. I've just discovered that my barber has been their director all along, and that he's a cardinal in the Roman Catholic Church to boot, and that he in turn answers to you. And you—to whom do *you* answer? I gather it's not to the pope. What should I say to you?"

The Cardinal's "v" smile only became more pronounced, looking almost engraved into his face. "Well, of course, I answer to the Holy Father. What sort of Catholic cleric would I be if I did not? On the other hand, I do hold a rather privileged position here—you must understand, I have seen every one of the popes come and go in my time. *Every single one.*" He waved a hand as if brushing aside something quite inconsequential. "And I could have been pope myself, had I desired—and remained pope for centuries, too. That would have given the world something to think about, would it not? A deathless man in the same office for century upon century. Such a miracle would have astonished millions. Think how impressive that would have been. It would have been much more impressive than the recurring births of Tibetan Lamas—something plainly visible and impossible to deny. But, as I said, I abhor the sensational."

He sipped from his glass.

"The sensational—the *miraculous*—lacks subtlety and it's dull," he continued. "Drawing attention to oneself, when there is important work to be done, is a bad habit—addictive, in fact. Such pride causes one to fall, you know. No, anonymity can be a wise choice in the use of one's power, if one has it. And I *do*—have power, I mean. Let me ask you. Had you ever heard of me before you were brought here?"

"No," I said. "I've never heard of you before. Which is odd, since my intelligence sources are pretty damn thorough. I have access to just about every state secret on the planet, but I never heard of you before today. You've sure got some influence over my most trusted people, though—my *formerly* most trusted people, that is. Just how in hell have you pulled it off?"

"Cardinal Silvestro has spoken to you about me at some length already," replied the Cardinal. "As old as you know I claim to be, and as experienced as I certainly must be to have impressed you, it would be more surprising still if I were not a man of great influence and, I might add, enormous wealth. After all, I've been in a position throughout history to accrue both power and riches. I invented means to do so as I felt necessary, moving adroitly through civilization after civilization, adapting myself to every changing context. I am by far the richest man in the world, for instance, though I personally try to live frugally and modestly. You will never see my name, however, on any register of the world's wealthiest. Yet I have the wherewithal to command nations. I have quite literally owned kingdoms and controlled governments. To be frank with you, I still do. But I keep myself hidden, behind the scenes. My power is all that much greater because of it. There is not an intelligence agency in the world where I do not have my influence, under a variety of different names, of course—and despite what you may have surmised from Cardinal Silvestro's explanations, I do mean it only for good."

I recalled the devil's words, spoken to Jesus in the desert:

"All this power will I give thee, and the glory of the kingdoms of the world: for that is delivered unto me; and to whomsoever I will I give it." Fieropasto was boasting now, of course, in much the same manner. But, I also sensed, he wasn't lying, and his sincerity resonated with me—all the more so, in fact, because I perceived in it the *realpolitik* that underlay it. It was something I understood very well.

"At any rate," continued the Cardinal, "my name has never appeared in any list of the Church's cardinals. I remain a cardinal *in pectore*. I've chosen to commit myself to a charity instead, which I exercise in private at my own considerable expense. Those poor men whom you've seen downstairs, who reside here, are the undeserving beneficiaries of that charity. And, also in private, I give myself to science."

"Science?" I asked. "You're a scientist? What kind of scientist?"

"Not intending to come across too proudly," he answered, "I'm a student of all the sciences—physics, chemistry, biology, zoology, botany, geology, meteorology, medicine... and so on. I have already mentioned that I know something firsthand about technology. I'm an inventor, in fact—although that's more of a pastime for me." He took a sip from his glass, and went on. "And I keep a private lab and a private museum on the premises. So, you see, I'm also a museum curator. No one, apart from myself, is admitted to the lab or the museum at present, but perhaps someday I'll relent and allow in some visitors of my choosing. Anyway, yes, I'm a scientist. I even tend to think of myself as the great, great, great granddaddy of all scientists. After all, I've had quite a few centuries to research and experiment."

I was hesitant to bring up what was unavoidably nagging at me, but I felt the time had come to hear it from his own mouth. So, I asked him outright: "Is it true that you claim to be the devil?"

He was silent for a few moments, as if pondering how best

to respond. He poured himself another drink before sitting back into the depths of his armchair and answering. "I would say that that depends on what you mean by the term 'devil.' If you mean, for instance, a satyr or horned 'god' with goat's legs and tail and all that—well, well, we're not children, are we? I'm no satyr or serpent either, as you can see. I feel no lust, have no interest in the carnal or the sordid, apart from a fascination with the psychology of those who are consumed by such things. Such people I make a study of, that's true. Thus my interest in the patients here. At any rate, I regard the occult, with which the devil is associated in the common mind, as a byproduct of human irrationality—occasionally amusing to watch from a distance, I suppose. Every form of 'Satanism' is a delusion of inferior minds. Only the deranged, the hysterics, the exhibitionists, and the gullible take it seriously. It's contemptible, frankly. As for possessions and exorcisms—well, most of those cases are accountable to mental disorders and hysteria. So, if any of that is what you mean by 'the devil,' then, no, I am not to be implicated in any of that."

"So, who or what *do* you claim to be?" I persisted. "Cardinal Silvestro led me to understand that you have identified yourself with the devil. If I've misunderstood…"

"That's something else entirely," he interrupted, mystifying me by this seemingly contradictory retort. I began to reply, but he held up a hand and gestured me to silence, and continued speaking. His demeanor all at once had changed. He no longer looked remotely self-assured or boastful, and he even appeared to be a little contrite.

"I do admit to being the one whose interference in this world has created so many misfortunes for the human race, and for that I have many regrets. Believe me, I feel quite bad about it. It was a grievous mistake on my part to involve myself in the affairs of this world—but I was young and inexperienced at the time. I was a rebel, as many young persons are at a stage in their lives. But I've paid for it amply since.

For one thing, it has left me in the unenviable position of being bound to the condition in which you find me here, no longer free to come and go as once I could. For me, life is a continuous house arrest." Here his voice took on the self-pitying timbre I had imagined it could, but I also have to confess that I was not unmoved by his plaintive words.

"However, I have made the most of it," he went on, smiling wanly, "seeking to make amends as best I can. This charitable institution, for instance. I've tried to rectify... well, everything, really. I've tried to rectify *everything*." With this last word, I thought I discerned a steely glint appear in his pale eyes, as if a blaze had flared up behind them for a split second and just as quickly vanished. He sipped his sherry, lost momentarily, it seemed to me, in a kind of reverie.

"So," I ventured after some moments of embarrassed silence, "what is it you want from me?"

"I think you know that already," he said. "I think you have already guessed what I want."

I sat silently and turned my eyes to the fire. Something in my brain seemed to catch a flying spark as I did so, as if the flames and my mind were for that instant a single living entity. I suddenly *understood*—and, as unsettling as the thought was, it actually made sense. *How* I understood all at once, I can't say, but I did. Perhaps Fieropasto had crept into my mind again without my discerning it and planted the thought there. But, yes, it made sense... I was, after all, the perfect choice.

"I think..." I began hesitantly.

"Go on," he urged. "I assure you that the thought in your head is one you can rely upon as on the right course. I know what's in your heart."

"Then," I said, "I think that *you* think I'm a candidate for the role of—it's crazy, but—for the role of *Antichrist*... '666' and all the rest of it..."

"Well, no, not exactly—but, you're on the right track, as I said," he said dryly. "I balk at all that stuff about '666' and

'Antichrist.' At the risk of sounding pedantic, that term 'Antichrist' is a complete misnomer. It's a term that shows up only a couple of times in your biblical canon, just in John's very short letters, and it never refers to a future political figure."

"Okay," I said. "I'll have to take your word for it. But you just now said that the idea in my head was on the right track. So, where does that leave us?"

"Your answer was partially correct," Fieropasto replied. "I do want those skills of yours as a leader to be employed globally for the welfare of the human race. And that could, I know, make it seem to you that I want you to play 'Antichrist' to my 'Satan'—but that's a matter of poor interpretation on your part, based on assumptions and associations you've inherited. Put all that aside. It's a matter of logic, really. Ask yourself this: Would the genuine devil, the real article, really be inclined to fulfill a prophecy that everyone in the world *already knew about beforehand*? Wouldn't he be clever enough to avoid doing the *obvious* thing, the one thing many are waiting to happen? Surely, he could read the Bible for himself, see the destiny foretold about himself and decide, 'No, I'm not falling into that trap.' Certainly, you must see how incongruous it would be for him to oblige the expectations of those he allegedly regards as enemies. I certainly have no intention of fulfilling any such so-called 'prophecies.' I'm an optimist on the whole—I have better hopes for humanity than that sort of thing."

He finished his sherry and refilled the glass.

"As for '666,'" he went on, "that was just an early Christian numerical cryptogram for 'Nero Caesar.' He was the first emperor to persecute the Church, you may recall. That supposedly 'mysterious' number doesn't have anything to do with a future 'Antichrist.' It's referring to Nero and the fear that he might somehow revive and return, perhaps under the guise of a new emperor, and persecute Christians a second time."

"Really?" I said. "How so?"

"Very simply, it's because the Greek alphabet, like all ancient alphabets, was a numeric system as well as an alphabet. Just like Roman numerals, for example. Hebrew is the same. In Greek, the letters that make up the name 'Nero Caesar' come out numerically as '666.'" He smiled again. "You see, you're safe. You're not Nero *redivivus*, so you're not 666."

I pondered all this for a few moments; then, I said, "Well, that's what crossed my mind. But now it seems I was wrong and you don't want me to be your Antichrist..."

"That's something of a moot point," replied Fieropasto. "I've explained to you what the 'Antichrist' is *not* and what the number '666' actually *means*. That's all. But let me explain myself like this. For centuries the world has desperately needed a leader who could guarantee peace and prosperity and justice for everyone. At the same time there has been resistance to that idea—fears that behind the smiling face would be the menace of tyranny and persecution. Fears of 'Big Brother,' you could say. So the word 'Antichrist' has naturally been bandied about, as if peace and prosperity and justice on a global scale would need to be in opposition to Christ—which is utter nonsense. The result of such fear-mongering has been that there are many, particularly in the United States as it happens, who distrust anybody who has risen to prominence or popular acclaim politically or religiously. The better the man, it seems, the more distrusted he eventually tends to be. Think of the pope, a good man with a worldwide influence. The result? People call him the Antichrist or the False Prophet. After all, the devil appears as an angel of light, or so we've been told. The point I'm making is this. The world badly needs to be healed. I'm largely responsible for its hurts. I've admitted that to you straightforwardly. And I have waited a long time for the right convergence of technology, historical crisis, and for the best-equipped man to lead the world and see to it that those hurts are cured. The time has arrived for this to happen."

"I know very well that the world needs peace and justice," I responded, "and I've committed my whole life to working for precisely those things. If that's all you wanted to say to me, then, fine, okay, I agree. But, seeing you've been so influential for so long, why don't you just assume the helm yourself? Why wait for me to come along? Or, maybe you intend to assume the helm through me, while you continue to keep yourself hidden from public scrutiny? Well, I'm not a person to be led. I'm not willing to be a puppet."

"I won't assume the helm, as you put it," he replied evenly. "That's not my position in this world. But, in any regard, I know you still have doubts about my claims. Of course you do. At this stage, you need it to soak in a while. Nor am I wanting you to be a 'puppet,' as you put it."

"I certainly do need to soak all this in," I said. "I can't force myself to believe it. I can go along with it—I mean, I'll humor you for now, but I can't suspend my disbelief further than that. At least, I can't yet. To say it bluntly, I've never believed in the devil at all. I'm not sure I can start now."

"Well," he sighed. "It probably shouldn't matter to me what you believe. Nevertheless, it does. Ah, well," he sighed again, as if his feelings had been hurt. "The fact remains that you're the best hope right now in this wretched world. I would like to die knowing the world is in good hands."

"Come on. Since when can the devil die?" I countered.

"Perhaps not 'die' as you understand the term. But, in fact, I would dissolve and have done with all this. And yet I don't want to disappear until I know that things here have been set right. Can you understand that much, at least? That would be my one consolation, to know that the consequences of my youthful destructiveness had been rectified at long last."

He rose from his seat and drifted across the floor to the window. Outside it was pitch black. Inside, the light was dim, and the fire had died down to a few crackling darts of flame here and there in the grate.

I looked at him standing there, a frail, pallid old man in scarlet, looking out into the night. I heard his peculiar high-toned voice, but he remained with his back to me. "I wish to know that what I brought about eons ago has been remedied—that peace reigns, humanity is in its right place, that everything is ordered—*really* ordered. No more chaos and mess. No more unhappiness and struggle. Just contentment. Just *that*. Contentment. Then, I can lay myself down and finally enter into oblivion. I deserve my rest, I think."

He stood there silently for another moment or two, then he turned slowly and sadly around and, with his face in shadow, said: "Have you ever read Dante?"

"Yes," I replied.

"I met him, you know," he continued, looking off into the distance. "A thoroughly unpleasant man, and somewhat plumper than he's usually depicted in art. At any rate, I met him. Here, in fact, in these very woods, and he stayed here for refuge for a few nights. He devised the layout for his *Inferno* here. And, given his sharp intellect and inside knowledge, he soon perceived who I was. When he did, he left in a great hurry, I can tell you, though he needn't have. I harbored him no ill will. I certainly wasn't going to betray him to his enemies.

"But he could show me no sympathy—much too prejudiced and not of an open mind where I was concerned. Even the pope—especially the pope, now that I think of it—couldn't sway him to perceive things differently than he did. Stubborn man. Well, be that as it may… there is one thing that he got right. Wishing no doubt to insult me, he described me at the end of the first third of his magnum opus as *stuck*—rendered immobile in the ice at the bottom of hell, cursed and left there, unable to do anything but bewail my fall. Well, he was right about the *immobility*, may he be

damned—the helplessness I feel, my sense of *being stuck.*
Somehow he intuited that." The slight whining tone had
returned.

"In what way are you *stuck?*" I asked.

"In this animal body, this human flesh and blood—I'm fas-
tened into it as tightly as Dante's devil was in filthy ice. That
hardhearted, rat-nosed little man knew it, and he mocked
my predicament, and he insulted me forever with his poem.
He never understood that what I bewail most is what I did to
this world, foolishly and youthfully, and what I want most
now is to see that evil undone. He saw my predicament but
not my tortured soul. Maybe you can understand the sense
of regret I feel, if nothing else."

I conceded that I could understand regret very well, thinking in that instant of Catherine.

"I do have influence and knowledge," he continued. "But
I'm not at ease with the idea of reigning directly. I don't
believe it's my privilege to do that. I prefer to use my influence covertly, through the numerous agencies available to
me. I'm imprisoned in a body just like yours, except for its
longevity. And when the time comes that I should die, it will
be true death, a final end. I wish to make amends for my
wounded conscience's sake, but then, what I really long to do
after that is accomplished… is *disappear.*"

"Are you saying that… God, I suppose… has imprisoned
you in a human body—that *this* is your hell?"

"That is one way of putting it," he said.

And then followed a long soliloquy. I reproduce it for you
below as best I can recall it. I'm not sure how it happened,
but by the time he finished it, I believed him to be who he
claimed to be.

He stood before the blackness outside, his back again
towards me, and—not directly addressing me—spoke in a
tone the effect of which on me was hypnotic. At times
visions of vast spaces and vague shapes I could not identify

flitted through my mind, and I had the unnerving sense afterwards that he had communicated these ideas directly to me telepathically.

The devil said:

XII

(The Devil's Soliloquy)

WHERE to begin?

God, naturally.

Perhaps it will surprise you to learn that God is a mystery to me. He hides his face from me. What is God? I do not know. I know that I—like everything else—live and move and have my being in God. His is the consciousness in which all creatures exist. Nevertheless, I do not know what God is.

Once, ages upon ages ago, I thought I knew. I recall a time, a time before time, as time is reckoned here, half-remembered as though through a fog, when I was free and could move with the speed of thought, when I was alive and unrestricted and could penetrate the insubstantiality of matter as if it were ocean spray. I remember how I was full of confidence then, how assured I was.

That was so long ago I can barely glimpse it in my memory now. At times I even think that, perhaps, it was only a dream. My sense of my own existence was vibrant, and I know I knew something then that I can't quite stretch my mind to know now, no matter how hard I try. I once could feel what it was to love and to be sharply aware. I was supremely aware of all things—I could see into them down to the roots of existence itself. Now, in contrast, I can barely feel anything at all. Acedia is my affliction.

And I believed I knew God then. God was inescapable, everywhere, in all things. He could not be perceived directly, even by my acute angelic senses. But senses were unnecessary. There were no words that passed between us. No words were

61

needed in that effulgence of knowing. I recall all this now as if through a glass darkly, so to speak. The bulk and weight of this flesh dims my memories. Yet once—once—I was a refined being. Not "immaterial"—there are many classes of materiality, after all, many types of "bodies," some grosser than others. My substance was light, in both senses of that word.

I cannot think of my former condition now, or of God, without a desire that I know to be without hope. It is the muffled recollection of something or someone once beloved, but now long gone. Except that the truth of the matter is that I'm the one who is long gone, lost, and dead.

My metamorphosis began with the appearance of this world. It stirred up something I hadn't realized existed within me—a love for the purity and cleanliness of refined and unspoiled perfection. This world we are now in, this imperfect world, with all its movement and wriggling and volcanic vomiting and organic growth, was an eruption, like the outbreak of something rank and fungal, a foul discharge into the unpolluted, ethereal, bright, and stable realms I had known hitherto. I watched with revulsion the self-ordering of raw, gross materiality, then the appearance of a low but living creation relentlessly emerging from the slime and the chaos. And I was appalled by it. It was monstrous in my eyes. Surely, I thought at first, this could not be the Creator's doing or wish. It must be some mistake.

I watched the advent of animal and human kind, raised up grotesquely from soil and muck, their forms changing in rapid succession, branching out and ceaselessly mutating, eating, always eating, and copulating, always copulating, and creating waste... and—in an instant of eternity, but in billions of years under this wildly riding sun—climbing out of its crude bestiality, I saw the ape become human, and I saw the evolution of a creature whose coming I could not greet. I knew from the start that none of this grand mess could ever become orderly—never rise to refinement and purity and perfection. It was all so low, dirty, hairy, violent, seminal, degraded and self-degrading. It stank and sweated and defecated and urinated and slobbered. It was marked and withered by the changing of seasons, and it died like the vegetation and the other animals, and rotted away. It procreated in ludicrous, bestial fashion—is there anything more absurd than the grunting and squealing and fleshy quivering of human copulation? This creature was slow and awkward and puny, and only gradually became aware of its superior simian intelligence. This creature—this human thing—disgusted me, and the more intelligent it became the more repellent it was in my eyes.

Was this smarter ape really God's creature? I wondered. Was this really his work? In dismay, I began to ask whether God—whatever God was—had died, and now this canker and corruption had appeared and was spreading malignantly. I don't recall by what stages I came to my resolve to put an end to it, but come to that resolve I did. But it was not going to be easy. In fact, I soon discovered that the job would prove too great for my efforts alone. The blight could not be eradicated entirely by me. That much was clear. There was a hidden divine energy working within it, pushing it inexorably up towards the light of eternity itself. And these human creatures... these pests... they were going to breed and multiply, regardless of what I thought of the situation.

Well, then, I determined, if I cannot stop their proliferation, I might at least manage to cultivate them. I might at least redirect their errant tendency from disorder to order, and tame their wild growth. That was my new aim—to tame this wild growth, as I say, to tidy it up and give it some much-needed governance. And perhaps, if I did all this, I might even develop an interest in it and study it, maybe conduct some experiments on it and learn what made it tick.

But, here was the burning question—where was God? Was there a God at all? Had I been deluded? Maybe, I thought, my memories of God were only imaginings, wishful thinking. I looked for God and could no longer find him anywhere. So I stopped looking. I thought one is only cheating oneself if one digs in empty graves. If God ever existed, he must have died, but perhaps he had never existed in the first place.

Or, then again, maybe I was God. Yes—that very thought struck me, but I dismissed it as blasphemous, as ego run amok. And yet—no one else seemed to be tending this bursting life, this explosion of myriad forms, this endless diversification of genera in all directions. Perhaps there was no "God" other than the races of "gods" of which I was both an individual and a singular species, that all this had happened spontaneously through no agency whatever, and that, without some concerted intervention, this unprecedented growth would continue to increase and expand and might possibly even overwhelm our pure empyrean. I was not alone in thinking this way, by the way—there were others who thought as I did. We gathered our forces, and I moved that something drastic be done—and I had their support. But what was there to do and how could we do it?

On this world, the human being was the solution. I quickly came to that conclusion. Homo sapiens were the most self-aware, the species with the most potential. This world had, as I say, caught my attention in particular—as other worlds had caught the attention of my co-conspirators. Something about this creature, man, fascinated me. He had promise. But he also evoked in me another reaction, not so detached, one that showed me another inexplicable side of myself that I had not known previously: he could be an amusement for me, a distraction from the malaise in my soul. I said that I was young then—and what I thought and did was foolish—the foolishness, you might say, of youth. But this wretched, annoying creature brought out the spite in me. To see this ape standing erect and learning to think was both an opportunity and an insult—an insult I took personally. It wasn't all annoyance *and pettiness I felt inside, I assure you. My better nature truly wanted to lift the creature up and give it some order in its miserable existence; but I likewise wanted to take it down a few pegs, humiliate it, and show it that it was no better than any other furry, disease-ridden, rutting animal.*

I swear I never touched any of the human creatures myself. Not then, not at first, at any rate. All I did—all, in fact, I ever needed to do—was to suggest certain ideas to them. The rest came naturally enough to these conceited brutes. There was no limit to the number of ways they found to destroy and degrade one another and the other creatures around them. I could whisper in their ears any vile or obscene or violent suggestion, and they would spring to it. These were the first of my scientific studies, crude in nature, I admit. I conducted my little experiments on them—some of them quite outrageous, in retrospect. I became fascinated at how the most vulnerable and innocent could be betrayed and vilely treated by their own kind. I observed unspeakable cruelty among them with a growing interest. And their impressive intelligence didn't limit their capacity to devise evil. It exacerbated it.

Do not judge me too harshly. I wasn't such a creature as these myself. I was of another order entirely. I was certainly not in the form you see me now. I was higher on the scale of being, in comparison to them, as Everest is higher than the Dead Sea—a poor simile, since indeed I was much more elevated still. I wasn't "moved" by their viciousness. I couldn't empathize or sympathize with them at all, even when I wished to see them improved. Mine was a pure intelligence—or so I thought. As it has turned out, I wasn't so pure or godlike as I imagined myself to be. Therein, my son, lies the kernel of my everlasting shame. Something in my treatment of these creatures was dragging my spirit downward. I found myself delighting in their sufferings and degradation. And yet I couldn't break my habit of observing human vileness; and, as I watched them adopt every suggestion I sent their way, I accommodated myself more and more to my degrading compulsion. The more foul they behaved, the more repulsive to my sense of refinement they showed themselves to be, the more they fascinated me. I was, as they say, enticed, hooked, addicted. And so it was that the more I experimented on the human animals, the more my own character fell and became contaminated by what I saw.

And then the unforeseen happened. I suddenly was one of them. I fell into a deep state of unconsciousness—something I had never experienced before and haven't since, nor had I induced it—and awoke from it to find myself in human form. Still, there was no sign of God, no divine word, no thunderous judgment from on high. Just this mute, but unmistakable, evidence of a curse, a condemnation, exile and humil-iation and loss—an imposed new condition, an imprisonment in a house of clay. I was condemned to go now upon my belly and eat the dust of this world. My mind was darkened, but my old shrewdness and skills, I quickly discovered, remained more or less intact.

To make a very long story short, though I was now reduced, yet like the parabolic prodigal I came to my senses. I had to get out of this place, but how? By reversing the effects of my previous interference? If that could save me, then, yes, I must try to bring that about. This became my only hope—to undo as best I might the worsening mess I had foolishly set in motion, to repair the damage I had done, and to do it by making use of the very race of creatures I had once despised but now had joined as one of them. By doing this, I reasoned, by redeeming them, I might at least earn the right to die in peace.

Yes, die. I don't wish to return to my former condition. I wish merely not to fall any lower than I have already. I want to give humankind its true savior, its peacemaker, and rightful governor. It can only be done through the proper exercise of benign power and firm governance and virtuous potency—not through meek ideals, high-sounding platitudes, mysticism, or lofty principles of selflessness. Those methods have been tried, *and the world is no better off than before. I want to die and leave the world in other hands—human hands, as is right. I want to give up, resign. I want to let go of all being, all life, everything—every thing—and dissolve into nothing. I only long for the purity, the cleanliness, of nothing. I'm so very tired, and so very sorry for what I have done.*

XIII

IT seemed as if a pall had fallen. I stared into a void. All the
color of the world seemed to drain to gray while he intoned
his recollections. Not really, of course—the light of the lamps
and the reddish glow radiating from the fireplace still shone
warmly against the polished mahogany paneling the walls.
Had anyone not party to our conversation entered the room
then, it would likely have appeared quite inviting and cozy.
But, for me, there was no warmth or color left in that room.
I have known depression in my life—the feeling that really, at
the bottom of it, everything lacks meaning and beauty. I was
feeling the weight of it now on my soul. A numb and drab
coldness seemed to permeate the atmosphere. The Cardinal
glided darkly across a blurred ashen landscape and resumed
his chair by the dying fire.

At last, with some hesitation, I asked, "What about all
those beliefs you stand for as a cardinal? What about Jesus
Christ? You say you want to redeem mankind and give it a
savior—those are the terms your Church gives to Christ."

"Yes, well, I am still uncertain what really to make of *him*,"
replied Cardinal Fieropasto with a wave of his pale, thin
hand. "I'll be completely honest with you about that. Despite
what you might care to think, I really and truly admired him.
I mean that. But, all the same, when he appeared on the
scene I had something entirely unforeseen on my hands. Yes,
I had known for quite a while that there were prophecies
about a coming 'messiah' and all that. But I had seen messi-
ahs come and go over the years, and I wasn't expecting anything astounding. Well, as it happened, I couldn't have been
more wrong.

"Jesus was a being in some regards not unlike myself, but disturbingly different in other obscure, mysterious ways. For one thing, whatever his ultimate origin, he really *was* human, whereas I was merely *stuck* in a human frame. I can't express the difference any clearer than that—it wouldn't make sense to you. At any rate, I was drawn to him, as everyone else was, and before long I became obsessed with trying to figure him out. He haunted my thoughts and troubled my dreams. You see, I thought I knew him of old. There was something familiar about him, but I couldn't be sure what it was. It was something like the exasperating feeling one gets when spotting a face in the crowd that he thinks he knows, but can't quite remember whose face it is. If I had ever known him before, I couldn't place him now. To make a long story short, I had to wonder about his motives. For one thing, it seemed that he had *chosen* to take on this low animal state, and it was embarrassingly obvious—at least, it was embarrassingly obvious to me—that he actually had an utterly incomprehensible *affection* for human beings. That was something far beyond my own capacity, for all my clinical concern for them.

"Well, I decided to offer to assist him. Believe me, it took some humility on my part to do that. I even condescended to make an attempt face-to-face. I was willing, you see, to provide him with everything a savior could possibly need to get the job done—self-realization concerning his mental powers, which were extraordinary—beyond my own, even. And I suggested he might enter into a close working relationship with me. I had already by that time acquired a lot of prestige and influence—I really could have helped him with PR, for instance, which he squandered away, as you know from the record. He was not proficient at making friends with, and winning over, the big movers and shakers of his day. I offered him unprecedented exposure and publicity, some real 'ins.' In short, he rejected every single one of my offers—every single one. And, if that wasn't ungrateful enough, he was haughty and proud, too high-minded for the likes of me, evidently, and he even had the cheek to throw scriptural quotes at me. Well, anyway, I admit I was stung by his rebuffs. I still am, when I think of it. At heart he was a rebel, too independent and idealistic. And he paid a heavy price for it, too. Those humans he loved so much did what they always do—they killed him in a particularly bloody way.

"He did rise from the dead, though, I'll grant him that. He said he would, and he did. Still, I've never been able to make head nor tail of that stunt. The Church tells the story in its own way—claiming that he's divine and rules in glory and will come back and all that. Sounds lovely and I go along with it for the institution's sake, but I can't see that anything has really changed since he came and went. Well, except for the Church itself."

"What do you mean 'the Church changed'?"

"The Church received the message about God's kingdom. But he was more of an ironist than his followers grasped. You know that Jesus spoke Aramaic, right?"

"Yes," I said.

"And that the writings that were collected and became the New Testament were written in Greek…?"

"Yes."

"Well, then. Both the Aramaic and Greek words for 'kingdom'—as in 'kingdom of God'—mean 'empire.' Jesus was using the term Rome used to describe its own empire. But he used it with a twist—I told you he was rebellious. He used it almost in a humorous way. What he was doing was thumbing his nose at everything Rome was trying to achieve through responsible authority, law and order, disciplined military, and all that. Jesus, on the other hand, wanted some vague, egalitarian, upside-down, topsy-turvy kind of 'empire'—an un-empire, if you will. You see the problem with that, I hope. It was a problem for me, certainly, since I had labored long and hard behind the scenes to get Rome to be precisely the empire it was when Jesus attacked all its principles and foundations. I concede he was a young man, after all. I know something about youthful zeal and rebelliousness myself, so I don't hold that against him. I wish he could have lived a longer life and outgrown his youthful enthusiasm. But, be that as it may, he flouted order, empire, and civilization when he rejected Rome, even though it was the one restraining force in that day against barbarism. He rejected, I say, to his own harm, a healthy coercion, which is the only thing that keeps human beastliness at bay..."

"I see your point," I said. "I'm a history buff and I always admired Roman efficiency myself, and even its judicious use of force. I took it as inspiration sometimes when dealing with rogue regimes. But, you realize, it was those same Romans who brutalized Jesus's people. You can't blame him for wanting something different."

"Yes, that's true," Fieropasto replied. "But let's talk *realpolitik* here and not the sort of idealism Jesus embraced in reaction to Roman force. Think how utterly charming the Sermon on the Mount sounds, for instance, but also how utterly impractical it is in the long run. The world isn't made better by turning the other cheek and loving our enemies. It wasn't a practical program of reform then and it wouldn't be today. Of course, we all know Rome had its flaws, but at least they were attempting, in admittedly primitive fashion, to shape their world for good. The Roman *pax* wasn't altogether a poor stopgap before something better could come along.

"Anyway, I set to work to undo the mistake Jesus had carelessly made. I determined to overturn Jesus's ideal of the 'kingdom of God.' I deftly and painstakingly subverted his message—bit by bit turning his bizarre off-track concept of 'kingdom' back onto the main road, *my* road. No more of this talk about becoming like children or serving one another or giving away one's wealth or being soft on the recalcitrant... Sure, keep that sort of pathetic language around for

71

those with more sentimentality than common sense, bring it out at Christmastime and for the youngsters, that sort of thing. But, ultimately, tame it and fit it into the old order. I don't care about whether the wineskins are old or new, to borrow Jesus's own metaphor, but I want to preserve the *old wine*, the wine I myself pressed out long ago. The problem, in my estimation, was never with the wineskins anyway, but with the 'new wine.'

"It took some doing to reach my goal. It became very much easier once I got Constantine and imperial power to adopt 'the faith.' But, for the most part, I've tamed that subversive message of Jesus. I've brought it step by step back into alignment with the governments and ideals of this world. His message had to be subverted for its own good, so that Christianity might not undo the sort of civilization mankind— and, in my own modest way, I—had worked so hard and for so long to establish.

"Jesus made slaves and children the exemplars of his kingdom. But, really, how tragically infantile that was—and from such an exquisite mind as his, too. But we know from experience, you and I, that only legitimate power and politics and even the occasional potentate are able to master human chaos. I make no bones about it—I side with hierarchy and law. I side with orthodoxy over heterodoxy and order over unruliness. I've seen too much human viciousness to believe that giving the mob too high an estimation of itself—even for its alleged good—is a good idea. You have, too. You know what I'm saying is true. Your record speaks for itself."

"And, the Church…?" I said. "How does that fit in here?"

"Ah, the Church. How thankful I am for it. The organized, imperialized Church has been a real haven for me. Jesus's ideas continue to live on in it, of course. That can't be helped. And, please, don't get me wrong—*merely as ideas* they're useful. There has been something quite unstoppable in their appeal and, like the mustard seed he talked about, those ideas have kept growing—sometimes wildly. I've been able, though, to rein them in, for the sake of mankind. I foresee, however, that they could break out once again and create disorder afresh—the potential is always there. Up to now I've been able to keep that danger at bay, keeping the hierarchy perpetually tied up with matters of theology and canon law and preoccupied with its own survival. Abstractions and minutiae and bureaucracy—with these I've kept the Church safe from the threat of Jesus's disruptive influence. I'm pleased to say that, for the past five hundred years, the hierarchy has owed more to the tough-minded realism of Machiavelli than to the dreamy, albeit well-intentioned, notions of Jesus. Niccolo was a frequent guest here, by the way. A pupil of mine, if you must know, although he really never quite believed the things he wrote."

"The Church says that Christ is God," I said.

"Yes," broke in Fieropasto. And now I saw a fleeting flash of anger in his eyes. "It teaches that. I can well believe that Jesus of Nazareth was somehow associated with the Creator, assuming that that great cipher exists. Both seem to me to be symbols of ineptitude, if you'll excuse the frankness. I've already told you I have my doubts about the Creator. He's certainly mad or bad or both. If he *is* out there somewhere, he has irresponsibly allowed this universe to get out of hand, out of control, and become unkempt. If Jesus is identified with *him*—and, of course, the Church has exploited that idea for centuries in order to unite the empire and to hold things together and to maintain its own order, and in that spirit I was happy enough to go along with it—but, I say, *if* Jesus is identified with God, we might also see in him the same ineptitude and disorderliness, reduced to a single, microcosmic human life. There is the same unjustifiable love of the unlovable. Not for me, thank you. In the end, I find the notion unintelligible. I give it lip-service for expedience's sake only."

I had never thought about these things in this way before, if I had ever thought about them very deeply at all. To be honest, I had paid such matters scant attention throughout my life. But I had to admit to myself that Cardinal Fieropasto's words struck a chord inside me. I could, among other things, understand his moral ambivalence. I knew in myself what it is to be an inexplicable mixture of goodness and evil, to feel concern and protectiveness on the one hand, and cool objectivity and even cruelty on the other. How often had I found myself, for example, justifying the laying off of employees because the company needed to streamline, knowing full well the hardship they would face, but managing to look the other way? In later years, I had sanctioned covert actions that meant the deaths or destabilization of entire populations. Terrible, but unavoidable. I had deployed troops, covered up plots and assassinations and interrogation techniques of the most ruthless sort, and in other instances stood by while injustice was done—simply because it wasn't in our national interest to intervene. I had made use of economic disasters that had in turn ruined the lives of innocent people. All these things I had done on the basis of *realpolitik*. I knew the exhilaration power gives, watching the results of decisions I had made while insulated and secure myself, sometimes even fascinated by the havoc I had wrought, though always justifying it as in a good cause. "Bad guys" had been eliminated and peace had been pursued—even though the latter was never fully achieved or for very long. An illusion of peace in some corner of the globe might even last for a few years when we got lucky. I had the resolve to oversee destruction, even feel satisfaction for it on occasion, and I knew how to remain detached through it all.

And then, I remembered that, as a boy of seven or eight, I had pushed a little girl of three with my finger so hard that she fell down; and when she got up, I had done it again and again, I don't know how many times. It had fascinated me to do it. It was coldhearted and it was cruel. I've never forgotten that incident.

In short, I realized then and there that I understood Fieropasto. He and I were not so very unalike. He had only said about himself what I, on a different level, might have said about myself. He felt concern for the human race, but also scorn. So, in my own way, did I. Despite his cool detachment and fascination with human viciousness, he still wanted to rectify the ills he had inflicted on human beings. Well, yes, I could understand that, too. His was a practical admission and a wish—grounded in solid, hard realism—for a viable solution to the mess. With that I was in accord.

And he was right, I thought, to note how unruly things had remained even after the one the Church called the Prince of Peace had come into the world. Jesus's teachings were beautiful, certainly, but—from the *realpolitik* position I had always espoused—they invited danger. What had Jesus actually accomplished to make the world a better, less chaotic, more humane place? In a way, I thought, couldn't it be said that all the world's governments were—and must be—"anti-Christ"? World leaders, to the extent that they were conscious of Jesus' teachings, would have to work against them just to get on with the business of government. How could one, practically, wage a war—even a so-called "just war"—and do so in accord with the mind of Christ?

Maybe, the thought occurred to me, that that's what theology had always existed to do—to get around the sticky problem of Jesus's teachings. Better to deflect their potential damage through obscuration.

So, even if—the thought revolved in my mind—even if I were now being drafted to be the "Antichrist," a term Fieropasto had waved aside as a red herring—what would I be doing any more unethical in nature than what I had already been doing and what had been going on for thousands of years? Why should the thought of taking responsible charge of such a disorderly mess as this world be shocking to me or to any rational person at all?

Was I, then, the elected "Antichrist"? And what would it matter if I were?

XIV

FIEROPASTO'S eyes had taken on a shade of glowing amber in the soft, flickering light of the room, and they had a curiously intoxicating effect on me. By no means am I excusing myself when I say this. Fieropasto had sowed seeds that were on the verge of taking root, and the soil had been prepared—I realized it now—over the course of my life. There was a peculiar force in him that stimulated my mind and conjured up fresh ideas. I was somehow "tuning in" to them and to him, and instead of troubling me, I realized they intrigued and coaxed me.

As if gradually rising from murky depths to the sunny surface of my consciousness, I became aware that some sort of hubbub could be heard outside the door of the suite. I heard shouting and then the sound of someone sobbing loudly, followed by running feet and a pounding on the door. Even the Cardinal appeared to be shaken by the noise.

With a look of annoyance he said vehemently, "Enter!"

Father Snithering stepped in cautiously and, it seemed to me, obsequiously, and bowing his wizened head, whispered something into the ear of the Cardinal.

Fieropasto rose slowly and said, with a note of exasperation, "Acting out again?"

"Yes," said Snithering, straightening up, seeing that secrecy wasn't necessary. "In the middle of the foyer, in plain view."

"And the dog?"

"Agitated, but alive and well…"

Fieropasto let out a sigh. "I think we have an incurable case on our hands with this one, Father. It's the third incident with him in the past month. It's really the last straw. Strict measures have to be taken. In fact, we had better halt his treatment altogether. Where is he?"

"He's downstairs now, in the foyer. We have him restrained."

"Come along," Fieropasto said to me. "You can observe what I have to deal with from time to time. It's the burden one shoulders when one tries to help people such as these."

The din ascended from the vast cavern of the foyer below, and we descended to where I saw a gathering of yellow-clad patients, all of them in a state of turmoil, some angry and some waving their arms and gesticulating and some of them wailing, and among this horde the black forms of priests in cassocks and male religious and nuns in habits, as well as other figures in the white gowns of medical personnel. It was a scene of chaos.

At the center of attention, around which all the others were teeming, was someone sitting—or, rather, contorted into a huddled mass—on a leather sofa. As Cardinal Fieropasto now bore down upon them with an energy that belied his years, the crowd parted and I recognized on the sofa the cringing form of Mr. Charlie—he of the frog's face and the gelato-gobbling dachshund.

He was wailing loudest of all, choking with immense sobs, and then I saw, in the arms of a nearby sister, the trembling body of Cerberus, the little dog. A priest ran up to Fieropasto and said in Italian, "We took the dog away, but he came down in pursuit and tried to keep us from taking it from him—violently. He struck Sister Prudentia very hard with a nutcracker."

"I didn't hurt him," whimpered Mr. Charlie, meaning the dog, I presumed, and looking up imploringly at the Cardinal who now stood bending over him. "I didn't. It was a game we played. Just a game."

"You hit Sister Prudentia!" shouted the priest. "With a nut-cracker—a heavy metal nutcracker…"

"I didn't mean to hurt her!" wailed Mr. Charlie. "I didn't! It was an accident! She tried to grab Cerberus by the tail and it made him yelp and I was trying to save him from getting his tail pulled…" And the rest of his defense was impossible to make out for the choking sobs he emitted.

Fieropasto stood stolidly over him. "Brother Drogo," he said to a corpulent man wearing what I learned later was a white Dominican's habit, but not taking his eyes off Mr. Charlie, "Take the dog there from Sister and remove it to safety." Then to the sister who was holding the dog, who turned out to be the wounded but seemingly stoical Sister Prudentia, he said, "Are you all right?" She nodded, handed Cerberus to Brother Drogo, and slipped off somewhere out of my sight.

Mr. Charlie continued to whimper. Fieropasto knelt down beside him and gently laid a hand on his shoulder and muttered some soothing words in his ear in what sounded almost like a singsong voice, even perhaps like a lullaby. I couldn't make out a word of it, standing as I was in the background, feeling uneasy. The fat Brother Drogo meanwhile carried the trembling little animal away. Mr. Charlie, seeing this, let out an unearthly howl of mingled rage and grief.

"No! No! No!" he bellowed. "Cerberus! Bring him back!"

Fieropasto grabbed Mr. Charlie by the shoulder, more roughly now, and forced him to turn and look him in the eyes. He locked his gaze on Mr. Charlie, and continued to chant to him in the same low singsong tones.

Mr. Charlie stopped his wailing, his eyes growing wide and wet. "We were only playing," he whined. "He wanted to play. He liked it. He liked it…"

"Not another word," said the Cardinal firmly, their eyes still fixed on each other's. "It's enough now. No excuses, and don't blame the dog. You will make your confession and you will spend time in solitary reflection. Do you quite understand me?"

Mr. Charlie broke down and began to sob. "Yes," he managed to burble. "I'm sorry, I'm sorry, I'm sorry. Please forgive me. Please forgive me. It won't happen again. Please bring him back…"

He went on like this, and Fieropasto motioned to a priest, who immediately took Mr. Charlie by the arm and escorted him through the now hushed assembly and from the vestibule. The last I heard from Mr. Charlie was: "Cerberus liked to play. He wanted it. Where will you take Cerberus?" And then he was gone, his pleas and whining steadily diminishing until there was silence.

Fieropasto came over to me, Snithering at his elbow. "If you will wait here one moment," said the Cardinal, "I must speak a moment to the head nurse." He turned to a gaunt nun in medical attire standing a few feet away and they spoke together in lowered voices, Snithering still at the Cardinal's elbow. When Fieropasto parted from her, I heard him tell her in conclusion, "Just get him prepared. Downstairs."

During those few brief moments, while Fieropasto, the gaunt nun, and Snithering had their backs to me in consultation, I felt someone at my left shoulder tugging at my sleeve to get my attention. I turned to see a short, rather young man standing there, another Dominican as it turned out, with a swarthy complexion and a five o'clock shadow, and—when I turned to him—he hastily shoved a piece of paper into my hand and, before I could utter a word to him, he scurried off and officiously began herding patients toward the stairways and elevators.

I looked down at the scrap of lined notebook paper he had put into my hand, torn diagonally from a larger sheet, and read what was scrawled on it in blue ink and underlined three times: "I must speak with you later. I will find you. 888. Brother Antoine."

I put the paper in my pants pocket, wondering what "888" meant. Was it a room number? It was a conundrum I had no time to ponder there and then.

Well, then, I'll just let Brother Antoine find *me*, I thought. I won't worry about it.

My headache was making a comeback.

"It is very late," said the Cardinal, having come back over to where I stood. "I must leave you now and allow you to rest and think. We can speak again tomorrow. And now, Father," he said, turning to Snithering, "please lend me your hand."

Fieropasto, who only moments before had seemed so vigorous and imposing as he parted the crowd like Moses parting the sea, now took the arm of Father Snithering and allowed his secretary to half support him as he made his way towards the elevator doors. He suddenly looked reduced, shrunken, and feeble, drained of energy.

As order was being restored in the grand foyer, I slipped away to the elevator and headed back to my suite. For some time I lay awake in my bed, the day's impressions replaying themselves dizzily in my mind: the frog-like wailing little man and his traumatized dog, the Cardinal's singsong lullaby voice, the obsequious Father Snithering, fat Brother Drogo, the gaunt nun, the short Dominican and his scrawled note, not to mention Fieropasto's strangely enticing words to me earlier, the disquieting atmosphere of strangeness—even creepiness—that permeated the vast edifice, all those weird inhabitants in yellow, and the sense that (no matter what anyone chose to call it) I really had been *abducted*, merged and danced and twisted and pirouetted inside my head. But, at long last, sometime in the wee hours of the morning, I fell into a fitful sleep.

XV

I AWOKE to the resonant "bong bong bong" of a church bell. My window was open a little so as to catch the fresh air, and there was a chapel outside. Slipping from my bed I went over to it and looked out. The bell tower was about a stone's throw from the window, visible now in the somber morning light. It was a separate stone building, set among the trees, and not very large. I had caught only a brief glimpse of it the day before during the tour with Snithering.

I looked at my smartphone, which I used as a timepiece and alarm clock, though it had been rendered useless for anything else, and saw that it was half past seven. Breakfast, I had been informed, would be served at eight, and I was expected to join Cardinal Fieropasto in his private refectory, along with Cardinal Silvestro and Father Snithering. I got myself ready and at five minutes before eight, Snithering rapped at my door. He led me to the elevator, and once inside we descended to the very bowels of the enormous, shapeless asylum, down past and below the grand foyer, all the way down to the bottommost floor far underground, where Fieropasto made his home.

Stepping from the elevator behind Snithering, I found myself once again looking about me with wonder. I hadn't been brought to this level of the building the previous day, so the sight that met my eyes now was new to me and, indeed, staggering. We stood in what appeared to be an enormous crypt. The high vaulted ceilings were very high indeed—I judged them to be something like 115 to 120 feet from floor to ceiling. It was windowless, of course, but brightly lit by lights suspended many feet overhead. The decor was mostly

Gothic, but not without additions (more like intrusions to my taste) from the Baroque era. It all indicated vast wealth, also evidenced by its rich furnishings, numerous and enormous mounted canvasses, gigantic Baroque statuary (some of which stood a massive twenty or so feet in height), and acres of shelved collections of great leather-bound books. Extravagance, flamboyance, and curatorial pursuits were on display in these objects and many others besides. For example, at one end of this great hall—I call it a "hall" for lack of a more adequate term to describe the area—hung suspended from the ceiling by metal cables the long, curving skeleton of an ichthyosaur.

"This space dates back to the Etruscans," remarked Snithering as he observed me looking around. "Maybe earlier," he added. "Cardinal Fieropasto would know. He oversaw its formation. It has been shaped and reshaped over the centuries—there was none of this vaulting, for instance, until medieval times. Before that the ceiling was merely bare rock."

With that, he led me on past the wide range of treasures and through a large entranceway into the Cardinal's refectory. Here was a banqueting hall of grand scale, though nowhere near the size of the great hall we had just exited. Here were tables laden with dishes and enticing aromas from the breakfast that awaited our arrival. Immediately upon entering, my gaze was drawn to two paintings on the wall opposite me. I went over to look at them more closely.

"Goya," I said aloud.

Cardinal Fieropasto had risen from a large, throne-like chair at the head of the main table to greet me, and I saw Vic seated nearby. Both were resplendent in crimson cardinals' robes—the magnificent, overdressed style one sometimes sees in nineteenth-century oil paintings of indolent, sybaritic, and often bibulous Roman clergymen. Fieropasto came over and took my arm familiarly as I stood staring at the two appalling masterpieces. They had caught my eye because I knew both works and also because they seemed so out of place in a refectory.

"They are originals," said Fieropasto. "The ones on public display are copies—very good ones which I commissioned, of course. You recognize, no doubt, the one called 'Saturn Devouring His Son.'"

"I do."

In blackness, a wild-eyed, wild-bearded, cadaverous giant, sallow and horrible, was gnawing off the left arm of a decapitated pigmy of a figure, whose right arm had already been eaten, the blood flowing from the latter's nude carcass.

"An odd choice for a wall decoration," I said. "Particularly in a room where people eat."

"It is, I concede, an odd choice," said Fieropasto amiably. "But I see it as an ascetical selection—a disincentive to gluttony. Gluttony is, after all, the first of the seven cardinal sins. The one that caused your first ancestors such difficulty, as the old story goes. The other piece is an earlier work of Goya's."

"Yeah, I recognize it," I said. "I've been intrigued by his work since I was a kid, when I first saw it in a book. Being a kid, the monstrous stuff in it grabbed me. Later on, I learned the historical background."

The second of the two scenes was quite different from the other, barely tinted in grays and pale pinks and beige. It depicted a courtyard in which there were a number of figures—some huddled, some staring, some gesticulating and grinning stupidly, some lying or crawling, the two in the center naked and apparently wrestling while a fully clothed man beat them with a flexed rod—all of them in the shadows under massive walls, above which gleamed a golden-gray sky.

"It's called 'Courtyard with Lunatics,'" said Fieropasto. "It's oil on tinplate. It creates quite an effect, don't you think?"

"It's very unsettling artwork," I replied. "Goya was a troubled man... there's a lot of his inner turmoil in these works, brought on by his times."

"I keep this one precisely for that reason," said the Cardinal. "It reminds me of the interior hell people carry within themselves. People like the patients here. People like poor Mr. Charlie. You might recall those lines Milton placed on the lips of his version of Satan:

> *The mind is its own place, and in it self*
> *Can make a Heaven of Hell, a Hell of Heaven.*

It's a sentiment with which I concur," he added, "even if I find his Satan much too passionate for my tastes."

"Mr. Charlie seems to have traumatized his dog," I said rather coolly.

"You have a passion for justice," said Fieropasto simply. I wasn't precisely sure why he said it, but apparently he took my comment as indicating that quality in me. "A strong man—a true leader—needs that streak in him," he went on. "A bit of steel in the backbone is an admirable quality. King David displayed the same trait when Nathan told him the story about the rich man with the many sheep, who had taken his poor neighbor's lamb and made a feast for his visitors with it. He became angry on behalf of that poor man."

"David had also just committed adultery and murder, I believe," I said. "Not exactly the behavior of a just man, I'd say. David doesn't come off looking too good to me."

"You know your Bible?"

"A bit. It's pretty rusty," I said.

"Still, you must agree, David's sense of justice also pushed him to accuse himself just as sharply as he accused that rich man," countered the Cardinal. "He was a just man right to the end, despite himself."

"I suppose you could say that," I replied. "Still, on his deathbed he guided Solomon to put all his enemies to death. David seems pretty ruthless there. Not that I don't have some sympathy with ruthlessness when it's a necessity. But he seems to have gone too far with it."

"Think how much more effective his ruthlessness might have been," said Fieropasto, his mouth briefly forming into his v-shaped smile, "had he possessed your company's weapons technology. The sort you employed so often while you were in office, for instance."

I had no reply to make to this, not knowing what he was getting at by the remark. Feeling my face flush a bit, I brought the discussion back to the Goya pieces. "But these paintings... they're very depressing. Don't they strike you as depressing?"

"They remind me, as I said, of the terrors and turmoil in the minds of the men who live here. That courtyard is rather like the foyer upstairs, I think. People dazed, confused, haunted... And Saturn eating his son—look at that bestial old giant; why, he's just mad—not evil. He's driven to cruelty by madness. He destroys what he loves in order to stave off death. What a terrible weight he carries in his madness. Poor Saturn. Poor Francisco Goya, for that matter. The men upstairs, though... well, they hurt what they loved, like Saturn in the painting here. They did horrible, brutal, depraved things—to the innocent, the undeserving. But they were mad. And don't for a moment think that love was altogether absent."

With these words, he smiled sadly, as if moved by their plight. But I couldn't tell if his was a sincere pity or not. For my part, I felt nothing sentimental in my heart regarding those who abused children.

"The cat loves the canary, too," I said. I could see that he appreciated this retort, but I couldn't tell why.

I was spared trying to come up with anything more to say because, at that moment, Father Snithering drew up alongside us and remarked, "Breakfast is served."

The meal was sumptuous. There was certainly no sign of asceticism in its bounty. Conversation was innocuous and Cardinal Fieropasto played the convivial host. Vic said little all this time, but I noticed that he appeared watchful of me. Snithering also said little and ate nearly nothing, but his eyes roved and darted about the room as we ate. When I spoke, I made small talk about the décor, the immensity of the refectory and the rest of the underground crypt. And soon we were done.

"Walk with me a bit," said Fieropasto to me after we had left the table, once more taking my arm. "I will show you my orchids in the hothouse. 'They are nasty things. Their flesh is too much like the flesh of men. And their perfume has the rotten sweetness of a prostitute.'"

"Pardon me?" I said.

"Just a couple of lines from *The Big Sleep*. I like Raymond Chandler," said Fieropasto. "Have you read him?"

I said I had a long time ago and that, being an old movie buff, I liked the Bogart film.

"Philip Marlowe is a bit of a moralist," said Fieropasto. "A little like you, I think. I don't disdain that quality, mind you. But, don't mind me. Just digressing. Come now and see my orchids, 'rotten sweetness' and all."

We left Vic and Snithering and headed up the elevator and through the foyer, and out into the courtyard of the immense structure. The vast rambling stone edifice, half buried among great limbs of towering pine, loomed above us, and we made our way past the chapel to a large greenhouse that stood not far beyond it. We entered the greenhouse, Fieropasto carefully latching the door behind us.

The interior was stiflingly hot and damp and, as soon as the door shut, I felt as if I were trying to breathe through a wet towel. All about us was a contained tropical jungle of fronds and leaves and vines, alive with blooms. The fragrance— which he had very adequately described with his quotation from Chandler—dominated the atmosphere.

"It's always a pleasure for me to come in here," remarked the Cardinal. "It's a secret garden for me, a patch of Eden, into which I can creep away alone and find solace. I have little use for growing things or for most animals as a rule. But, for some reason, I enjoy these orchids."

We meandered through the greenhouse, oppressive with its heat and pungent atmosphere, the Cardinal caressing an orchid here or bending a stem there to inhale the fragrance of a bloom.

"Some say orchids are parasites," he said. "In fact, they're epiphytes, you know. They frequently grow on top of other plants in the wild because they must in order to survive. You must admit they have a remarkable appearance."

I said I could see they did, but after some minutes in the hothouse I was beginning to feel faint. It was, I could see, a leisurely stroll for him, but for me it was fast becoming a perspiring and gasping experience. He showed no sign of strain and didn't break one bead of sweat. He was oblivious, as well, of my own discomfort, so rapt he was in his plants.

Finally, stifled to the point of wooziness, I said, "I need to step outside and catch my breath."

"My apologies," he said, looking slowly up at me with a dreamy expression on his sallow features. "I sometimes forget it can be rather uncomfortable in here for most people. I'm someone who thrives in extremes, you see. I like it either intemperately hot or downright icy. A peculiarity that came with this body of mine."

We emerged from the greenhouse. I was soaked through with perspiration, which intensified the feeling of coldness for me as we stepped outdoors, but, thankfully, that served to revive me. I found a granite bench beside the chapel wall and sat down, mopping my face, but enjoying the bracing wintriness on my cheeks. The Cardinal, looking cool and dry, sat beside me. He cleared his throat, and the sound of it seemed somehow portentous. It was a signal that digressions and chitchat were over.

"You are here," he said somberly, "because at this moment

the world is at peace, but it won't stay that way for long. You and I both know what is brewing out there and where it all could lead. Southeast Asia isn't stable and Africa is about to explode in numerous places. Eastern Europe is experiencing new tensions. The Middle East... well, you know that the Middle East is always about to erupt. You know the brutalities that war and uprisings bring about. Mutilations, torn limbs, blinded eyes, bodies crushed or slowly suffocating, people burned or buried alive, mass rape and repeated rape until a woman's insides are destroyed, the slaughter of children, the violation of children, the injuring of children, starvation, exposure to the foulest diseases, slavery, imprisonment, torture, utter and thorough dehumanization on all sides... You know what I'm talking about. You've seen it. There is no end to the sheer horror, the murder, the misery, the cruelty that human beings perpetrate against other human beings. They always claim that elevated ideas and causes lie behind their depredations, but, in the end, their causes stink like the decaying bodies they leave behind. These things are happening or on the verge of happening all the time—*all the time*. Whatever vileness and perversity the human mind can imagine—to ruin, maim, degrade, and torture, on grand scale or small scale makes no difference—it practices in abundance and with delight. 'The wickedness of man is great in the earth, and every imagination of the thoughts of his heart is only evil continually.' 'The heart is deceitful above all things, and desperately wicked: who can know it?' You know the song. You and I could discuss these things endlessly, but it would be pointless. You know it all already. You also know it has to end. You know further—do you not?—that only a visionary leader, a realistic man of justice and an unsentimental seeker of peace, who won't hesitate to do what he must, can do the job. You are now poised to take that position, if you will have it."

He sighed and looked off into the distance.

"All the military elite of the world awaits a leader they can get behind. All the peoples on the planet await peace and prosperity, and they want to rally behind the man who can achieve these ends. Every intelligence agency on this planet is at my disposal, as well. They can be at yours, if you will take them. My centuries of life and influence have seen to that. I hold the reins of authority—and you can, too. You've seen what I can do. I brought *you* here, for instance. That shouldn't have been possible according to the rules of the world you thought you inhabited. But all along you have been living in *my* world without knowing it, and the rules are, in fact, rather different than you imagined. *My* rules—and *your* rules, too, if you have the nerve to uphold them with firmness."

I merely nodded, taking in his words. I no longer doubted that real power lay behind them.

"At the risk of sounding terribly melodramatic, your destiny is to assume that role. You don't have much of a choice, really. I know it sounds like a cliché, but you were born for this, and everything in your life has led you to this precise and perfect moment. In a few days you will be receiving the Nobel Prize in Oslo. That will be your opportunity, the day you can speak up and make your proposal to the world. They will hear you then. I assure you there will be immediate enthusiasm for it. People are hungry for a real leader, a real father figure for all the nations, someone who will care enough to be gentle when gentleness is needed, but tough enough to do the hard things when toughness is required. The great nations will trust you—you've given them every reason to do so. Your passion for justice, as I noted this morning, is well known to everyone. You're essentially a man of peace, even if—with regrets—you have directed the shedding of blood. This sad world is weary of conflict and it wants peace. The governments, the militaries, the intelligence forces… all are primed and ready for you."

I noticed, as he spoke, the short fat Dominican brother with the five o'clock shadow, the one who had thrust the note into my hand the previous night, exiting the chapel. He glanced over in our direction and then hurried off towards the grand edifice. I thought of his note, still in my pocket: "I must speak with you later. I will find you. 888. Brother Antoine."

The Cardinal continued: "I have informed Cardinal Silvestro that he will take orders from you from this day forward, and that you shall be apprised of every detail, every contact, and everything pertaining to our whole network throughout the world. I will soon be departing, getting out of your way, and I'll leave you to guide things in the right direction. But, in the meantime, I will see to everything you will still need from me. All *you* need to do is step into the role prepared for you. And, if you are absolutely honest with yourself, you know that you really haven't a choice in the matter."

"What do you mean, I 'haven't a choice'?" I shot back. "I think that's my decision to make in the end. I need to mull it over and then I'll let you know what I decide. But I've got to do the deciding."

"Now, now, listen," said Fieropasto evenly, seeing that I was a bit ruffled by his words. "Don't get me wrong. You have a choice in the strictly volitional sense. But you haven't one in a moral sense. It's a choice between doing what's right or shirking a heavy responsibility—the heaviest in the world, in fact. If destiny is something more than mere projected fantasy, you haven't a choice to go against your very self, and you are a moral man, a genuine moralist as I indicated earlier to you. Look squarely at your own life, all those presentiments and premonitions of yours, those occasional intuitions that told you that your life was extraordinary in some way, driven by a purpose that could not be countermanded. You could always feel the inexorable pull towards something great in yourself, coming from wherever it came from. You have always known that you're meant to be a 'great man,' a predestined man. You've felt it in your very bones every day of your life. No, I think you know the dice have been cast and you have a vital role to play. Unless you step into that role, the evils of this age will compound. 'There will be wars and rumors of wars' for many years to come. You can—and you *must*—ensure peace. It's your duty."

Well, he had moved something deep inside me with that. It was as if he looked into my mind and knew all my secret thoughts. I had always felt what he described: a deep, abiding sense of my own importance in global affairs. It wasn't the case that I merely suspected that I was extraordinary and, at least for the time being, indispensable. History had conspired to put me in precisely that position. It had been serendipitous and unplanned, synchronicity playing its hand at every perfect moment, as if the cosmos itself was open and yielding itself to me. I hated the notion of "destiny"—that word had been used so often and abused so much. Yet, secretly, I had to admit it fit my circumstances and the whole, implausible course of my entire life. Fieropasto had indeed struck a nerve.

But I said, "Surely, it won't be as easy as you imply."

"No," he replied. "It won't be easy. I won't lie to you. You will need to draw on that sense of justice you have. There will be resistance. Conflicts will occur here and there—of that you can be sure. You will need to use your military and police and intelligence forces and your most efficient technology. There will need to be—I hate to say it—prisons and detainee camps. It can't be accomplished without a modicum of bloodshed, as sad as that always is. You will need to have a will of steel and an unbending conviction that, in the end, peace and security will be had. But they *will* be had, and that very quickly—perhaps only in three years or so. You have shown such fortitude in the past. You can do it again."

I was beginning to feel a chill now, the effects of the tropical greenhouse environment on me having dissipated in the December air.

"But I see now that you're cold," said the Cardinal, looking at my trembling shoulders. "I can also see that you're weighing my words. Good. They have struck a necessary chord in you. You can resonate with the truth of my assessment of your situation. It has touched your conscience. Mull it over, then, but don't take too long. Now's the time to act."

He sees right through me, I thought to myself. Surely I'm not so obvious as all that...

After a short pause, he assumed a solicitous tone and said, "Why don't you go inside, or visit the chapel? Get warmed up. I intend to remain here a while longer."

Without another word I rose and went back towards the house, cursing myself for the conflict of feelings inside me. I walked away from him, on the one hand wishing that my life had led me in some other direction and yet, on the other, thrilled that it hadn't.

And indeed it hadn't, and I was beginning to believe that Fieropasto was right, and that I was a man whose destiny must be shouldered. Not as an act of ego, but as an act of responsibility. And who was to say, even if Fieropasto were the devil incarnate and all his intentions were really destruction and mayhem (which I doubted), that I should be guided by those intentions? Fieropasto could die. He had admitted as much. If I could step into a role of actual authority, commanding the arms and personnel and technology to subdue the worst and, in the bargain, ensure peace and justice in the world, even if it meant facing down opposition, would I not also be in a position to oppose even Fieropasto if that should ever become necessary? He had spoken as a man about to make his exit, anyway, and into my hands he was placing the whole apparatus he had labored for centuries to create. I could use it for good, whatever his intentions might be—and good was certainly what I wanted. He was right that I was, and had always been, a moralist. Whether or not it was what he really wanted, I couldn't say, although I was inclined to believe him at this point; but, if it weren't, would it really matter in the end if I were the one holding the reins?

This was the call of duty reserved to great men. I was, I already knew, a great man, an extraordinary man, and a just man, and fate had put me in a position unlike anyone who had ever come before me. I might have wished for an alternative path, but... in fact, no, not really—I did not wish for an alternative path.

XVI

AT noon I was served lunch in my suite, and afterwards I took a short nap. I was left to myself throughout the afternoon, and around three o'clock I decided to stretch my legs. I went outdoors again and strolled the grounds near the chapel and the greenhouse, where I had earlier conversed with Fieropasto. These buildings and two or three others (sheds for tools and equipment, I judged, from the look of them) stood in a fairly expansive clearing surrounded by dense woods. At the edge of the woods, not far removed from the greenhouse, I noticed a path meandering among the trees. As I strolled along it, lost in my thoughts, I gradually became aware of the sound of rapidly moving feet behind me on the trail. I turned and there, running after me and gaining quickly, was the short Dominican brother who had surreptitiously passed me the scribbled note the previous night.

He stopped in his tracks the instant he saw me turn around, just a matter of feet now from where I stood. He was wearing a luridly purple parka over his white habit and white sneakers with orange laces. He nervously looked around him in all directions and—satisfied that no one else was about—strode up to within a few inches of me.

"I'm glad I found you," he said breathlessly in subdued tones. "I'm Brother Antoine. I'm a Dominican, by the way…"

"Ah. Like the inquisitors," I said, attempting vainly to be humorous. He didn't register it, but went right on with his introduction.

"I've been posted here at Cardinal Fieropasto's estate to keep an eye on things and report back to the CDF."

"The CDF?" I said.

95

"The Congregation for the Doctrine of the Faith. It's the dicastery at the Vatican that..."

"So, I was right," I said. "That's what used to be called 'the holy Inquisition.' I wasn't too far off the target."

He nodded with a vague look on his face.

"And you're here on their behalf?"

"I am. And I need to speak to you, if you can spare a few moments."

"All right. Well, we're both right here. What do you want to say to me?"

"Can we walk along nonchalantly for a little? I don't want to be suspected of telling you things I shouldn't."

"Are you likely to tell me things you shouldn't?" I asked.

He didn't answer the question, but said, "Can we walk along?"

"Okay, fine, let's walk," I said, and we proceeded down the path like old chums.

"By the way, I'm from Massachusetts," he said.

"Really?" I said, not caring in the least. "I noticed the accent," I added, hoping I didn't sound too apathetic.

"Lowell, to be exact." He gazed at me as if this information was particularly significant.

"That was Jack Kerouac's hometown," I said, not able to come up with anything else to say. "Ever read any Kerouac?"

"No," he said. "I stay clear of indecent books. I read philosophy and theology mostly—St. Thomas, Father Reginald Garrigou-Lagrange, that sort of thing."

I had read something in a magazine article about the Vichy regime not too long before that had mentioned Garrigou-Lagrange, but I couldn't remember clearly the details. "Wasn't he pro-fascist or something of the sort?" I asked.

Brother Antoine suddenly looked defensive. "Who? Fr. Garrigou-Lagrange? Well, you have to understand..."

"Never mind," I interrupted. "I didn't mean anything by the remark. Didn't mean to get off on the wrong foot. Sorry."

He looked stunned for a moment and looked on the verge of an expostulation, but he checked himself and went on about his mission.

"I've been sent here by the Congregation for the Doctrine of the Faith..."

"Right, you said that," I interrupted him again. Something in his demeanor made me want to be curt with him.

"Yes, yes. Of course." Brother Antoine now became flustered. I had been too abrupt.

"Why did the CDF send you?" I said, trying to put a little more affability in the tone of my voice.

"Well, to be absolutely honest, not everyone at the Vatican trusts Cardinal Fieropasto. No doubt you've heard his story, or at least his version of his story. You know he is... well, he is..." Brother Antoine's voice fell to a barely audible hush. "...The devil," he concluded, the agitation he was barely able to contain forcing his jaw to quiver uncontrollably.

"So I've been informed. I've also been informed that he has been intimately involved in the Church for centuries, that he's sorry for his past deeds, and that he's highly trusted among the hierarchy."

"And he's told you of why you were brought here, I assume."

"He has."

"And you're prepared to assume the role he has prepared for you? To be... the *Antichrist*?"

Brother Antoine, despite his nervousness, was unafraid to be blunt.

"We have discussed the meaning of that title," I replied in guarded tones, "and we both reject it as ridiculous. The same with '666'—it's a reference to Nero and doesn't apply to me."

"Oh, but there you are wrong," said Brother Antoine. "*Only to the extent* that it applied was '666' a reference to Nero. But it meant—and means—far more than any one particular historical personage."

"And '888,'" I said, remembering his note. "You referred to '888' in your message. What's that all about?"

"It's more numerology for you—for some reason, I thought you might understand the reference—or, at least, have your curiosity piqued by it. That's the numerical designation for 'Jesus.'"

We continued along the path. The woods were, in fact, a strange mixture of wild and tangled forest and a sculpture garden. The statuary was tantalizingly grotesque—a zoo in stone of whales and elephants and dragons and lions and tortoises. Among these petrified creatures, standing in stolid watchfulness or else contorted until their carved musculature looked like it might pop out of their ossified casings, were the figures of Aphrodite and Triton and Proteus and—again—Saturn devouring one of his offspring, and many others. All gigantic and intended to astound and flabbergast, no doubt, and dating back to who knows when; a veritable horde of monstrosities and deities and semi-deities half overgrown by vines and creepers.

We paused beside a vine-covered, chipped, and armless statue of what appeared to be Hercules. The fat little man pointed a finger up at it, and then looked significantly at me.

"This statue is older than the designations '666' and '888,'" said Brother Antoine. "We know from the iconography of the period that this is probably Hercules. The hair and beard, the naked torso, the draped shoulder... it's all recognizable. There's no mystery about the statue. Likewise, there's no mystery about '666' and '888' for those who know where to look. The Church Fathers wrote about these things, and anyone can read what they wrote. Cardinal Fieropasto told you only part of the truth."

"But there's more," I said with a sigh, looking up at Hercules. "There's always more."

"Yes, and I'm duty-bound to tell you the truth."

"Let me guess," I said. "In order to persuade me not to

take up the role—to prevent me from being the Antichrist and '666'..."

"Good heavens, no," interjected Brother Antoine, looking shocked at the very idea. "No, no, no. *Not at all.* Quite the reverse. I'm here in the name of the dicastery to *encourage* you to take on the role and hasten things along to their predetermined end. You have a predestined duty to do that. I wouldn't think of trying to prevent you."

I let that statement sink in. I said nothing, staring dumbly into the ancient marble eyes of the statue.

"So... what you're telling me," I said after some moments, "is that the CDF—the Vatican—*wants* me to assume the position of Antichrist. Is that what you're saying? Am I getting that straight?"

"Yes."

"To be, really and truly, '666'—that's actually what you all *want*...?"

"Yes, yes. It's your appointed role."

"...To usher in the end times, the last days, the apocalypse... and the return of Christ. I think I get it. If I say yes to Cardinal Fieropasto, then—as you suppose—Christ must return soon..."

"Well, not the 'apocalypse'—that word simply means 'revelation.' Technically, it doesn't refer to an event. But, yes, as for the rest, that's precisely what I'm telling you. At least in essence."

"And the Vatican *wants* this?" I said again, still finding it hard to swallow. "Shouldn't the Church be trying to *stop* me? If not for the sake of the world, at least for the sake of my own soul? I mean, if the Antichrist is supposed to be a really terrible guy bent on evil—"

"He is."

"Well, if he's really so terribly evil, shouldn't he—*shouldn't I*—be persuaded by you to repent and *not* to go down that particular road to my own perdition?"

"I trust that you are *not* making light of this," Brother Antoine cautioned.

"I assure you I'm not," I replied. "I'm merely taken aback that the Vatican would wish me to unleash on the world all sorts of plagues and carnage and, in the end, to go to hell. I assume you must literally believe everything that's in the book of Revelation."

"We believe it. The point is not whether or not it's true—it's a given, it's predestined to happen. The 'son of perdition' must arise and lay waste the earth and reign, at least until he's ousted at the end. Armageddon and all that—all true. And all the indicators are that you are the one to step into that role. Personally, I'm sorry to tell you, you're already lost. That's a matter of divine providence and predestination. You can't kick against that goad. No one in heaven or earth can change what the Lord has decreed or alter your personal destiny. But you can hasten the events, and—just perhaps—and here's the point of my coming to you now... just perhaps you might consider sparing the Church too many miseries during your reign. Mitigate its sufferings, I mean, leave us with our property and our lives unmolested... That's what we're asking of you. That you proceed to the next step and assume your predestined office, but that you temper your diabolical actions with mercy. Mind if I smoke? I'm feeling a bit nervous."

"Sure. Smoke. Have one of your death-sticks, why don't you. That'll kill you, you know. Killed John Wayne. I'll take one, while you're at it."

He handed me a cigarette and I took it. He lit his and I noticed his hand trembled as he did.

"So, help me to understand what you're offering me," I continued, more intrigued than I had any reason to be. "A pact of some sort?"

"We would prefer to call it a 'covenant'—the word 'pact' has bad overtones," said Brother Antoine, picking a bit of tobacco off his tongue and coughing slightly. "You know, a 'pact with the devil' and all that—doesn't sound good, does it? Or 'Axis Pact,'" he added, in perhaps somewhat sarcastic deference to me.

"No," I conceded, "'pact' doesn't sound good. A 'covenant,' then—with the Antichrist?"

"Yes, if you want to put it that way."

"You can't be serious."

"Let me explain myself, then. I will tell you all I've found out here. You, of all people, have a right to know."

"And '666' and '888'—you will, I hope, enlighten me further about these, uh, ciphers."

"Yes, I shall. You should know who you are and exactly what it is you represent."

And so, in those dark woods, cold, moist, and vaporous, seated on the marble base of a crumbling Hercules, the little brother from the CDF mingled his cigarette smoke with the surrounding scent of wet fallen pine needles and rust-brown leaves, and told me a tale of espionage in Satan's lair.

XVII

IT had been five years since Brother Antoine had been sent from Rome by the Prefect of the CDF to keep an eye on things at Cardinal Fieropasto's estate and to report back about him on a weekly basis. The Vatican is a small city with a variety of offices and dicasteries overseen by all sorts of professional ecclesiastics ranging from the ambitious to the phlegmatic, from the downright lazy and stupid to the crafty and cunning to the very nearly saintly. There had long festered among some of those holding high office resentment towards Cardinal Fieropasto, just as he had many who doted on him. To be fair to the Prefect of the Congregation for the Doctrine of the Faith, he was himself not personally envious of Fieropasto. He was truly troubled by the strange reports that had proliferated over the years concerning the goings-on at the Cardinal's estate. His worries were linked to his more general anxiety regarding the failed policy of covering up clerical scandals involving the abuse of minors. The Church's reputation had never been so precarious as now. So, what on earth was really happening behind the walls of Fieropasto's charitable asylum for such perpetrators? Rumors had been leaked in dribs and drabs from the inside for decades, but never enough to accumulate any solid evidence of malfeasance. Not all, but certainly a disproportionate number of the men in yellow housed at Cardinal Fieropasto's estate had been clergy. For example, Brother Antoine told me, the name "Mr. Charlie" was a pseudonym for a particularly nasty example of the type. The latter had, in fact, once been the powerful Metropolitan of a large American city, all set to get the cardinal's hat in Rome, when his transgressions with underage boys had come to light. Even as Brother Antoine told me this, I recalled the story, now some years past. I recalled "Mr. Charlie's" younger, vigorous features in the news, and found myself shocked at the marked deterioration of the man that had occurred since. Formerly he had been an imposing, celebrated, articulate figure, and now he was reduced to a crumpled and whining wretch who had to be separated forcefully from a small dog to ensure its safety.

At any rate, the Prefect had become increasingly uneasy about Fieropasto's patients and his experiments in innovative care techniques for them. He was also, needless to say, dubious of Fieropasto's personal character. "The devil is the devil," he had said to Brother Antoine behind closed doors. "Can a leopard change his spots?" The Prefect said he needed a spy at the estate, someone trustworthy and of impeccable character. Brother Antoine was the perfect choice, in his estimation, just the sort of unprepossessing and, therefore, easily ignored person who was the right fit for such espionage. Brother Antoine, pudgy and dull-looking, was surprisingly fearless and capable of countenancing gross horrors without quailing. He was also a Dominican friar, very much a traditionalist (so much so that he even regarded the Second Vatican Council as a mistake and distrusted the current pope's "liberal" tendencies). He was the kind of man who—had he lived in a happier time—might have been a fervent supporter of Torquemada. He was trustworthy, in other words. So his superior had him embed himself as an informant in the household of Cardinal Fieropasto. There he had remained for the past five years.

He had singled out and ingratiated himself with Father Snithering during the first year. The latter hadn't many friends, but, after some initial suspicion on his part regarding Antoine's carefully rationed kindnesses, he grew more and more relaxed with him. After having received from Antoine occasional small gifts of fine cigars and cognac for his birthday and at Christmas, and endeared by unlooked-for sympathy for his arthritis and an apparent shared interest in his passion for vegetable gardening, Father Snithering eventually became confident enough to entrust Antoine with a set of keys to Fieropasto's apartments—including his personal laboratory and museum—in the monstrous, labyrinthine crypt below ground. Getting old and stiff in his joints, Snithering had long desired a helper he could trust to give him a hand in his duties, which were basically those of a secretary and butler. Since Fieropasto in turn trusted Snithering, he also trusted Snithering's choice of Antoine as an assistant. So Antoine found himself close to the inner circle in that mammoth compound, with keys to areas and passageways reserved only to the elite of the elite, and all this because he was deemed harmless.

All told, achieving this high level of trust had taken the better part of three years. During that time his reports to the Prefect had been brief and perfunctory, with not much cause for concern regarding the Cardinal's residence and its strange set of patients. After all, it had been efficiently run for centuries, the men who were kept there were guarded and never let near children, and they received—and had ever since the 1950s—ongoing therapy from psychiatrists as well as spiritual guidance from confessors.

As soon as Antoine had been entrusted with the keys, he had taken to exploring the Cardinal's crypt whenever Fieropasto was away, as he was on occasion. Invariably, when the Cardinal traveled, Snithering went along with him, and Antoine had the run of the place and the means of access to every nook and cranny.

At first he ventured stealthily into the main rooms that made up Cardinal Fieropasto's living quarters: the great room with its magnificent vaulted ceiling, the dining area, and the Cardinal's private sleeping quarters. The last of these revealed a frugal taste in accommodations. There was nothing Baroque in style to be seen in there; no artwork adorned the bedroom walls, not even a crucifix, and the atmosphere was somewhat stuffy. A single canopied bed, a side table with a lamp on it, a straight-backed chair, and a roll-top desk were all the furnishings the room contained. The roll-top desk was locked, and Antoine did not possess a key for that.

The only door leading into the laboratory and museum complex beyond was in Fieropasto's sleeping room. On his first visit there, Antoine had tested the lock and found that he had a key among those entrusted to him that opened it. But he had not passed the threshold and had exited the crypt. On his second visit, however, which he made a few weeks later, he unlocked the door again and this time went in.

What met his eyes was an expanse of crypt even more awe-inspiring than the high-vaulted area behind him. It extended for what seemed miles in all directions. Unlike the brightly lit section on the other side of Fieropasto's sleeping room, however, this region was dimly lit with lights of a muted amber color. Antoine took in immediately that this not only was a very different space with very different décor from the other, but that there was—or, at least, he claimed to have felt—a profoundly sinister quality there for which he was entirely unprepared.

"Sinister?" I broke in as he told me of his discovery, leaning back against Hercules and smoking a second cigarette. "What about it was sinister?"

"I don't know... something," replied Brother Antoine, his voice quavering. "The smell, for one thing..."

"The smell?"

"Like urine and ammonia... It was very pungent."

"You said there was a laboratory in the vicinity. Maybe the noxious odors came from there. What else?"

"There were large glass cases, but I was too far away from them to see what they contained. But..." he lowered his voice to a whisper, "I could have sworn they contained mummies, upright bodies... *human* bodies. Like in a museum, on display—you know, display cases. But they were unlit and I couldn't see them clearly enough to be certain."

"What sort of a spy are you?" I said. "You didn't go in and investigate?"

"No."

"Why not? You might've found they were ancient relics or something, nothing to worry about..."

"Well, I didn't. Maybe if you'd been in there, you wouldn't have wanted to do it either."

"Maybe not," I replied. "Okay, go on. What next?"

Brother Antoine had proceeded no further on that occasion and, in fact, never ventured deeper into the larger area at all, despite the fact that he returned repeatedly to the zone just beyond the door leading from Fieropasto's bedroom. But, on that very first occasion, he had discovered in that zone an alcove, not far from the door, which he explored before beating a hasty departure. As I said, he was to return to it time and again in the coming months—though he never strayed too far from the doorway to go further into the sinister, malodorous area deeper inside. The alcove was similar in its dimensions to the Cardinal's sleeping quarters, he told me.

What he had found there, numerically labeled and lined up on sturdy oaken shelves, was a cache of diaries, leather-bound, and numbering more than four dozen, all penned in Latin in the spidery handwriting of Cardinal Fieropasto. He began to read them, taking in as much as he could. What he discovered there, or so he told me, he had subsequently related to the Prefect of the CDF. The result of his intelligence had been alarm, even panic. The Prefect took the matter directly to the pope. The pope, having no one else to turn to, took the matter to God.

Brother Antoine continued to make visits to those diaries over the following year, memorizing the material and recounting it at the Vatican. Alarm turned to fear and trembling in high places. Ancient texts and historical records—apocalypses, pronouncements, prophecies, recorded locutions of Marian apparitions, and the ponderings of theologians spanning the centuries—were scrupulously consulted. The Vatican's most secret "secret archives"—those archives that officially do not exist—were opened and ransacked for information and confirmation. The dossiers concerning Cardinal Fieropasto were examined in minute detail—from the first mention of him in a second-century account of the life of Simon Magus to the present day. One document, Brother Antoine told me, had been stolen from a monastery library in Egypt in the 1890s by two enterprising English adventurers, and then sold to the Vatican for a large sum of money. There it had remained ever since. It appeared to date back to the sixth century. It bore the title (in Greek), *On the Reclamation of Satan*. Brother Antoine explained to me, that the treatise was an extreme, radical defense of the idea of *apokatastasis*.

"*Apokatastasis* is a Greek word that means 'complete restoration,'" explained Brother Antoine. "A harmless word in itself—it shows up even in the Sacred Scriptures. But, unfortunately, it came to refer to a heretical notion that, in the final restoration, everybody would be saved and healed—including *the devil*." He paused dramatically to see what effect that bit of news would have on me.

"Okay, so…?" I asked, exhaling a stream of smoke into the chilly air.

"It was a speculation allegedly propounded by the third-century theologian, Origen of Alexandria," said Brother Antoine. "He was one of Christianity's great early thinkers, but he went off the rails with that nutty idea—assuming he really proposed it. Some say he didn't, but, well, anyway… If he did, he committed the fatal error of proposing an absolutely all-merciful deity."

"I can see where that might be a problem for the Church," I remarked.

"Origen's problem," said the diminutive Dominican, "was that he simply didn't know where the love of God ends." He followed this with a wince of distaste, flicking his cigarette butt to the ground and stepping on it with a passionate vigor that seemed to say, "Thus to all heretics!"

"The Cardinal's diaries," I said. "What about them?"

"I will tell you only two things about them," replied Antoine. "The first is this. Cardinal Fieropasto truly desires peace for this world. If he tells you that—"

"He has," I interjected. "I tend to believe him."

"Well, he means it. But—he is, let me be clear, *godless*. Not an atheist, mind you, but godless. Perhaps that's a difficult distinction for you. Never mind. He doesn't believe in the return of Christ, he has utter disdain for any notion of a competent Creator, and he simply wants to die. I've never read such despairing words as his. To read his diaries is the most depressing and disheartening reading you can imagine. He wants to cease to exist—he doesn't want eternal life or heaven. He simply wants to dissolve and be no more forever. Before he goes, though, he wants this planet and humanity in particular to be reduced to a squalid, base existence."

"I thought you said he wanted peace."

"Well, yes. But, let me put it this way. Based on everything I was able to read, I'd say his concept of peace on earth is stasis. No dynamism, no more growth, no more illusions of 'something better' or 'something exalted' or 'something sacred' or 'something spiritual.' He wants all this striving and growing to stop. He feels robbed of a spiritual existence himself, he feels that his essential purity was compromised with the material universe's creation, and he wants to leave it—at least here on earth—in a state of going no further. He wants *nothing else to happen here* until the world's end."

"So, you're telling me that's what he really wants," I said. "And he wants me to help him do it."

"Yes, well... but *we* know differently."

"Who is 'we'?" I asked.

"The Church," said Father Antoine. "We don't believe you will bring peace on earth at all, but war and famine and persecution. We're banking on our belief that you will, because it will fulfill the prophecies and Christ will return in glory. At any rate, Fieropasto also knows that peace can't be won without bloodshed and an iron rule."

"So, Cardinal Fieropasto wants me to bring about peace, and you want me to bring on all the horrors of the 'Great Tribulation'? What if I told you I have no wish to do anything of the kind? I'm not a monster in disguise. Sure, no war can be fought and won without bloodshed. That's the price we pay for freedom in an imperfect world. But what makes you think that's what I want or what Fieropasto wants, either?"

"You'll do it nonetheless, whether you want to or not. It's your destiny, I'm sorry to say. I'm sure you don't want to bring down horrors on the earth. But that's what *must* occur, as it's been foreseen. It's been revealed. The peace the Cardinal wants is, as I said, stasis. A world purged of spiritual endeavor, reduced to political, business and financial concerns, a language that lacks sophistication of thought, a technology that keeps people pacified, and a preoccupation with sex and noise and sports. The Cardinal's world will at least be partially realized. It already has been to some degree. He thinks he knows what he's doing. He refuses to recognize himself in the Christian portrayal of the devil. He calls it all 'rubbish' and 'lies' and—and... But, never mind all that. At any rate, he uses the most appalling scatological language for the ancient prophecies. Look, here..."

He produced from his parka a piece of paper. "I copied and translated this directly from his Latin text, from one of his diaries. Just listen to this..." He unfolded the paper and began to read: "'They all want Jesus back. Well, he isn't coming back. He left—the one bit of good sense he ever displayed—and why would he ever wish to return here? They all live in a delusion that I work incessantly to dispel.'" He refolded the paper and tucked it back inside his parka. "Okay, so there you have it in a nutshell. The Church believes that Christ will return and the devil will be thrown into the Lake of Fire. I know it sounds tough—but I believe the devil has no chance of redemption. Fieropasto is without hope. He will burn eternally. Oh," he suddenly exclaimed, "I'm sorry!"

Apparently, he suddenly had recalled that I, being the Antichrist, must likewise be tossed into the Lake of Fire along with the Old Dragon. I ignored his exclamation of regret.

"So," I said, "assuming you're correct, I'm destined—*predestined*—to fulfill the devil's will."

"Yes," said Brother Antoine. "And we're begging you in advance for clemency. Please be lenient in your persecutions. Practice moderation, although you must do what you must do. And please, please spare the Vatican and the properties of the Church around the world, if you can, until the Lord returns..."

I wasn't feeling like a predestined persecutor and mass murderer as I stood there out in the woods, puffing on a cigarette and gazing distractedly around me at the grotesque statuary. His plea for only moderate mass murder and preservation of ecclesiastical real estate didn't make much of an impact on me at the time.

I said, "You mentioned that you would tell me about two features of the diaries. You've just given me one. What's the other?"

"The second feature has to do with what he's written about you."

"Me? Well, of course I'm curious."

"You are aware of your Hebrew blood?"

"Yes," I replied, wondering where this was leading.

"If the diaries kept by Cardinal Fieropasto are correct," said the little priest in hushed tones, "—and he has, in fact, kept a record of your lineage that goes back before the birth of Christ, and even before the birth of David—then you have a bloodline that can be traced to the Tribe of Dan. Not exactly 'Jewish' blood; not from Judea, that is, but *Hebrew* blood, Israelite blood, Danite blood."

He gave me a significant look, arching his eyebrows in what would have looked to anyone observing us like two men plotting a conspiracy.

He must have noticed I wasn't picking up on his implications, as evidently he supposed I should.

"You read old books," he said.

I nodded.

"Sir Thomas Browne—does that name ring a bell?"

"Yeah. I had to read some Browne in college," I replied.

"You might recall, then, that Sir Thomas Browne mentioned in his *Religio Medici* that it was said of old that the Antichrist was to be born of the tribe of Dan."

Admittedly, I recalled no such thing, but I nodded anyway.

"If you look carefully in the Apocalypse," Antoine went on, reassured by my feigned assent, "you will note that, in the seventh chapter, it is the one tribe that's not included among the redeemed Israelite tribes of the last days—it's not listed among those who make up the symbolic number of the 144,000 Hebrew believers."

"Oh, ah," I said.

"I'm talking about an ancient Jewish and Christian belief regarding the Antichrist. One can find it, for instance, in *Adversus Haereses*, which was written in the Second Century by Saint Irenaeus of Lyons. He got his information directly from Saint Polycarp, the Martyr-Bishop of Smyrna, who in turn got it from the Apostle John himself. The belief has persisted for centuries. For example, it shows up in the late fifteenth-century Irish *Book of Lismore*, but very much elaborated upon there with all sorts of nonsense. At any rate, it's a long-held tradition, and Cardinal Fieropasto insists in his diaries that it's true. And, what's more, he has meticulously traced your genealogy back to the Danites, in fact to Samson himself. It seems he fathered a child through one of his dalliances with a prostitute. Your ancestor."

"I remember Victor Mature in the role in the movie," I said, trying to bring a note of levity into the discussion, although I wasn't feeling at all lighthearted. "Somebody asked Groucho Marx what he thought of the picture and he said he liked it but couldn't help noticing Victor Mature had bigger knockers than Hedy Lamarr."

The Dominican didn't so much as crack a smile. He remained somber, looking troubled. "You should know that Cardinal Fieropasto has manipulated your career from the beginning, throughout your whole life, beginning with your years in university, then in Albuquerque with SNARC, the World Bank, the U.N., your presidency... He's been the shadow in the background of your entire life, pulling strings, making deals on your behalf... You wouldn't be in the position you're in today without him. He's been your 'godfather,' so to speak, your patron."

"Well, all I know is until I was brought here I'd never heard of him."

"Maybe not. Doubtless you have seen him, but only as a face in the crowd, perhaps someone in an audience, a priest seated in business class on an airplane a row away, that sort of thing. His money was there whenever you needed a donor, passed through the hands and identities of others. He supplied you with many of your employees. He steered your presidential campaign, for instance, more than you could possibly suspect. And, of course, he controlled your intelligence and security forces. He's been with you every step of the way. More than that, he was on personal terms with members of your lineage going back centuries. It's all there in the diaries."

"Members of my lineage, eh? Like who...?"

"Charlemagne, for example. Pope Alexander VI—Alexander Borgia—, Louis XIV of France, Grover Cleveland—all in your lineage. Numerous others, both great and small." Brother Antoine looked at his watch. "Look. I haven't got a lot of time left. The point is that you've been in Cardinal Fieropasto's back pocket all your life—right up to this crucial point in history. He set you on your predestined course, unveiled your fate to you, and now you will take your appointed role. It's the unalterable will of God, although that's not exactly how Cardinal Fieropasto would see it."

"Then, I suppose, I'm immeasurably in his debt," I said. "Insofar as my life has had meaning, I owe it to him. Thank you for letting me know how much I owe him."

And I meant that, truth be told. For if what Brother Antoine was telling me were true, then there could be no other inference. It was now a matter of obligation to a bene-factor. And that I was the man for the position I had little doubt. If Fieropasto had, in fact, been responsible for my election, grooming, and even the material means of my rise—albeit anonymously—then he had managed it well. I have always known that I have enormous resolve, the capac-ity to make tough decisions, even to the point of eliminating obstacles ruthlessly when required, and that I stood philo-sophically in my determined pragmatism with other leaders of the past—Churchill, for instance, just to name one exam-ple. My record speaks for itself. When the job must be done, I have the will to do it. I'm willing, too, to answer to my con-science later. One learns to live with that and continue, despite one's qualms, simply to live.

And what was it that Nietzsche had said about Goethe? "Goethe conceived of a strong, highly cultured human being, skilled in all physical accomplishments, who holding himself in check and having reverence for himself, dares to allow himself the whole compass and wealth of naturalness, who is strong enough for this freedom... a man to whom nothing is forbidden, except it be *weakness*, whether that weakness be called vice or virtue." Well, perhaps I'm not skilled in all physical accomplishments, but, as to the rest, those qualities apply to me. And now, I asked myself with Hercules looking on, was this a time for weakness or a renewed resolve? Was the time for a just and ordered world peace come at last and was I set on a course to usher it in?

XVIII

I STOOD up. Brother Antoine did likewise. The late afternoon's shadows were lengthening and the discomfort I felt from the chill and damp of the woods had been growing for some time. I wasn't a young man anymore, and every joint was stiff and my back ached from the marble shinbone of Hercules, which had been pressed into it for more than an hour.

Standing and stretching my back now, and stamping out the last cigarette on Hercules' toe, I asked, "So, then, what is it the CDF wants me to promise the Vatican? Give it to me in concrete terms."

"Exactly what I've said already," replied Brother Antoine. "Exercise leniency. That's the Holy See's request. The end of times must come, but you can exercise mercy to the Church, sparing her people and property."

"Nothing more specific?"

"Not yet. We could keep a channel open between the Vatican and your regime, a back channel if you prefer. What we'd like is some sort of ongoing cooperation with you, an agreement of some kind we could reach amicably. All we want now is your assurance that we can be allowed to get through the coming times with a modicum of impunity. Perhaps we could pay some sort of tax in exchange for protection, if you wanted that. It's in your hands. All we can do is ask."

"Maybe," I said, "you've misjudged Cardinal Fieropasto's intentions. It seems to me that everything he's done he's done to serve the Church. And maybe you've misjudged me."

"That's the subtlety of the thing, isn't it?" said Antoine. "I mean, if you thought of yourself as being capable of doing evil you wouldn't be the sort of man the world would naturally trust. Your belief in your own rectitude is what Cardinal Fieropasto counts on. If you would observe him more closely, though, you'd begin to see that he wants to reproduce his character in you. He believes in his own rectitude, just like you. His self-righteousness is so completely mixed up with his malevolence that they've become one and the same. He sees in you a tendency to assume the moral high ground, even if the assumption is based on pretty flimsy evidence—and that's his own tendency. He knows you have it in you to dish out what you think is justice without showing any mercy when you're pressed to the limit. And he also knows that you *will* be pressed to the limit. You've done it before and he's calculating you'll do it again."

"Well," I said with impatience, "maybe things won't go as you predict. You seem pretty damn sure I'll unleash some unholy catastrophe. Fieropasto, on the other hand, seems convinced I'll bring peace on earth. What makes you believe your scenario is right and his is wrong? Because, if I *could* bring about peace on earth and never persecute anybody in the process, and if this 'peace' wasn't just the paralysis and stagnation you told me Fieropasto wants, then what could you possibly object to in that? But, look, if it's any consolation to you, I give you my word right here and now that I'll show you and the Holy See and anyone else who wants it clemency and no persecution and no horrors. Okay? Will that satisfy your superiors back at headquarters?"

"Well, we'll just have to trust you on that."

"I'm not a murderer," I replied as evenly as possible, my irritability mounting. "Whatever my past actions have been—and some of them have been regrettable, I'll admit that, okay?—still, should the thought disturb you, Fieropasto won't be deciding my every step in the future. I will. So, you have my word. You don't need to worry about Fieropasto if I'm the man in charge."

We were now sauntering back down the path in the darkening woods towards the compound.

"You asked about '666' and '888,'" said Antoine as the clearing and its buildings came into view.

"Yes," I said. "What about it?"

"The number '888' refers to perfection," said the Dominican. "It's the numerical value of *Iesous*—which is 'Jesus'—in Greek. Look here." He stopped in his tracks, took a piece of paper and pencil out of his pocket, and wrote: "*Iesous* = I (10) + e (8) + s (200) + o (70) + u (400) + s (200) = 888." He handed it to me.

"Impressive," I muttered.

"Eight is a significant number in early Christian thinking," he continued. "There are eight sides on the traditional baptismal font, for instance, corresponding to the eight persons saved on the ark of Noah and also to the 'eight days of creation.' The early Christians called the day when Jesus rose from the grave 'the eighth day of creation.' Now, follow along with me here..."

"Do I have a choice?" I said, feeling weary of the whole conversation and wanting it to end. But I gave him my attention anyway as we paused near the chapel, feeling it was the least I could do.

"St. Irenaeus is clear that the number '666' refers to the *recapitulation* of human evil in the person of Antichrist," he went on, leaving me even more confused than I already was. "Six is the number of man—man was created on the sixth day in Genesis, for example. The Antichrist—the Beast whose number is '666'—sums up and embodies the great sin of all mankind. The Apocalypse puts it like this: 'let him who has understanding reckon the number of the beast, *for it is a human number.*'"

He stressed those last six words, eyeing me sharply. I tried to look interested in this mumbo-jumbo. He continued: "Don't you see? *Three* 'sixes' means 'six'—the number for mankind—*taken to the extreme*: man who will attempt to rule over himself, man who has created a succession of empires in history, who subjugates and makes war and crushes other kingdoms. Certainly Nero was one such 'antichrist.' There have been many 'antichrists' throughout history. *The last one,* the *final* Antichrist—*you*, in other words—will recapitulate on a grand, global scale all that has preceded you. Yours will be a rule of iron."

"So," I said, "let me see if I'm following all this. You're saying that '666' refers to my quality and character."

"Yes, I'm afraid so," said Antoine, suddenly looking nervous. "It signifies your future. You can't help being who and what you're foreordained to be. Sure, you seem tame right now... But that isn't going to last once you're running things. It's been foretold and it's unalterable."

We were standing before the chapel entrance. "I'll leave you here," said Antoine. "I'm going in to say my office. Remember our talk and your promise. I'd say 'good luck,' but somehow, under the circumstances, that scarcely seems appropriate."

He turned on his heel and went inside. I couldn't have guessed it there and then, but the next time I would see Brother Antoine he would be virtually unrecognizable to me as the same man.

XIX

AS you may have deduced, my impression of Brother Antoine throughout the course of our conversation hadn't been encouraging. If anything, my patience with him had not only not improved the longer we talked, but had declined sharply. The more he expatiated, the more I preferred Fieropasto's directness—even when I didn't fully understand the latter. I had no doubt that Antoine believed everything he had said to me; that, in fact, he fully expected me to commit the grossest depredations imaginable and that I was—or was destined to be—nothing more than the devil's puppet. He clearly imagined me capable of leading the world to Armageddon, of wholesale slaughter, of ruling over a subjugated humanity with oppression and persecution, and so on. In my opinion, he had no clue about me as a real human being with real feelings. How, I wondered, could he picture me so gracelessly, as incapable of compassion and goodwill?

If you had been in my place, you might have felt scorn for him as I did. After all, if someone assumes that you're irredeemably evil and predestined to be so, not to mention eternally damned into the bargain, your reaction might well be— at least, I would assume it would be—to dismiss him as deluded. Antoine had been twisted, I felt sure, by centuries of superstitious fears and fanatical anticipation of the end times, by ancient documents filled with arcane symbolism, by prophetic puzzles and dubious apparitions, by a cultivated and exaggerated dread of diabolism and of "Lucifer." I won't bother to deny, however, that my opinion of him was colored by the prejudices of a lifetime.

By comparison, Fieropasto's vision was not so ghastly as

he made it out to be. To my mind, despite the implausibility—on the face of it—of his own claims, his wish that there be a firmly maintained rule of justice on earth was essentially modern, clear-sighted, and without pretense. He had, I felt reasonably sure, been honest with me. He hadn't minced words. Brother Antoine, in contrast, struck me as narrow-minded, doctrinaire, and all too willing to strike a deal with a person he considered the "devil's pawn"—in short, he seemed ready to discard even honesty if that would serve the interests of the institution he represented. Making a "pact" with someone he thought irredeemable and damned, a tool of wickedness, just to save his own skin and those like him and the Church's property—well, it made my own skin crawl to guess how low someone like him might stoop. Still, I resolved not to betray him to the Cardinal. He had, after all, entrusted me with his information, and I in turn would keep his secret. At least, I knew who he was, what he was up to, and where to find him should it ever become necessary.

So now what? I had made up my mind to continue my dialogue with Cardinal Fieropasto and to accept his proposition. But, I told myself, I would only do so on the condition that I would have full control of whatever future course must be taken. How I had come so quickly to regard this as the right thing to do, I can't say. I don't know why I came to that conclusion in so short a time. Looking back on it now, I see how incongruous with my well-known resolute character it was. I can only say this in my defense: Cardinal Fieropasto's implicit trust in me, combined with the information I now had concerning his benefaction toward me over the years, awakened within me an intuition I had long had about myself. I was, I felt, destined to occupy an unprecedented role of leadership in the world. That the way had been prepared for me and that all that was left for me to do was to step into the role fate had assigned to me seemed to be the crowning confirmation of my whole life's secret. It was a fulfillment and not an imposition on me. Fieropasto hadn't planted this self-awareness in me. He had simply opened my mind to the intuition I possessed already.

And, realistically, what else could I do? What other alternatives might I have chosen? Every decision I had ever made up to now had culminated in this moment of rare opportunity. Whether or not my life had been predestined, I couldn't say, but it certainly had been *post*-destined—every past turn on the path, every fork at which I had taken one route rather than another, had made each subsequent choice likelier than the one before it. And now I was on one single road heading in one single direction with only one choice left to make. I could see no other fork ahead of me, no side road, no alleyway. The way before me was, it seemed, so very obvious. The way that I had been "abducted" by Fieropasto—so easily, so quickly, somehow so *inevitable* to my mind now—indicated that I had been, and now was, in the hands of an irreversible fate. Was there an alternative? If so, what alternative? And, for that matter, why would I seek an alternative? And even if one had presented itself to me at that precise moment, following the protracted discussion with Brother Antoine under the shadow of the graven image of Hercules, I would very likely have ignored it as beside the point.

It was with this new determination, then, to continue my consultations with the Cardinal that I descended to the refectory that evening to have my supper. I had imagined that, as on the previous night, the Cardinal and I might retire to a private location, and there I would tell him that I was prepared to work with him, fairly certain that he would agree to my sole condition of absolute control—with him, of course, in an advisory capacity, at least for a while, should he desire it.

So, it was with some surprise that I found myself alone in the refectory. A very fine hot meal had been laid out for me, and Brother Drogo—the corpulent brother I remembered from the previous night—was on hand to serve me.

"Isn't the Cardinal dining this evening?" I asked as I seated myself at the table.

"Ah, no," Brother Drogo said, lifting the cover from the tray to reveal two succulent roasted partridges nestled among potatoes, carrots, and other vegetables and herbs. "The Cardinal regrets that he must be away this evening to attend to an important matter that's arisen. He told me you should be informed that he'll be back in the morning, and wished me to ask you if you would be so kind as to meet him tomorrow after the midday meal in your apartments? He should have some important news for you by then, he said."

"An important matter?" I asked, as the brother uncorked a bottle of Chablis and poured me a glass.

"So I was given to understand, sir," said Brother Drogo. "Rolls?"

"Yes, thanks. And Father Snithering and Cardinal Silvestro?" I inquired. "Have they gone with him?"

"Father Snithering always accompanies the Cardinal on matters of business," said Brother Drogo, placing a basket of hot rolls on the table before me. "I can't say where Cardinal Silvestro might be off to. He comes and goes quite a bit. It's rare to see him here on the grounds at all, really."

Well, of course, that made sense, I thought. Vic was in New York most of the year. I gave the matter no further consideration. I chose to focus instead on the partridges in front of me and to get an early night's rest afterward. I was fairly confident that tomorrow afternoon would prove momentous. Very possibly even historic. I would need my sleep tonight, then, for what I foresaw would likely be a lengthy discussion tomorrow, a meeting of minds, the start of making grand plans...

I confess that I felt growing excitement, even (and this I can't explain, since I'm not given to it normally) a sense of euphoria.

So I ate my supper with gusto, downed an uncustomary

third glass of wine, dabbed my lips with the white linen napkin, and, satisfied and inwardly glowing, went back to my suite ready for a full night's repose. All I missed was a good cigar.

What I never suspected, given my strange feeling of elation, was that my sleep would be drastically cut short by the reappearance of Vic, who came to me suddenly, bringing chaos in his wake.

XX

RATHER abruptly, I was fully awake. What awakened me, I couldn't say. I reached over to the side table by the bed and looked at the display on my phone. It was a few minutes past two-thirty in the morning. Looking over in the direction of the bedroom door, I saw that lights had been switched on in the outer room. From the angle where I lay I could see, extending from the seat of the armchair that Cardinal Fieropasto had occupied the previous night, the outstretched legs of a man in the full crimson regalia of a cardinal. The rest of the man and the armchair itself were blocked from my view by the door.

Ah, I thought to myself, Fieropasto has come back sooner than expected and is waiting to converse with me. I assumed he had awakened me with one of his mental tricks. Well, okay, I thought, I'm up. I'll go in and talk with him.

I switched on the lamp by the bed and slipped out from under the covers. I was wearing flannel pajamas, so I put on my heavy plaid bathrobe, tied it tightly about my waist, put my feet into my padded leather slippers and went into the outer room.

I was on the verge of greeting Cardinal Fieropasto when I saw that the man seated in the armchair wasn't Fieropasto at all. It was Vic—Cardinal Silvestro—who casually drew in his outstretched legs and stood up to face me. As I said, he was wearing the full crimson garb of his office and a red zucchetto on his dark head. When he stood up, he loomed over me and he seemed to my eyes to be much taller than usual. I chalked it up to a trick of the light—the lamplight was dim in the room and it cast distorted shadows on the dark wood of the walls. Vic's face, in that glow, looked even more cadaverous to me than normal, leaner somehow and more pointed. He looked, I thought, like a huge rook all draped in scarlet.

"Good evening, Mr. President," he said in formal tones.

"Vic, you surprise me," I replied. "Is there something wrong?" I said this because his look was anything but comforting. In fact, he seemed to glower at me menacingly, and I hoped his scowl was also a trick of the light.

"I want to show you something," he said in a low, faintly ominous voice. "Something you ought to see before you speak to Cardinal Fieropasto tomorrow."

"It can't wait?" I asked. "Perhaps we could see it together with Cardinal Fieropasto tomorrow...?"

"No," said Vic. He said that single syllable firmly, commandingly, as if there were to be no argument about the matter.

I started to protest, but something held my tongue. I suspect it was the severe look in his eyes, and the fact that he stood over me like a bird of prey in the black shadows.

Finding my tongue, I asked, "Okay, well, I guess... Where exactly is this thing you want me to see—now, after midnight? It's pretty chilly out here, you know..."

"Downstairs," he said. "In the crypt."

"I'm not dressed for that," I protested. "I'm in my pajamas and robe, as you can see."

"You're dressed as well as you need to be," he said. "Here, put on your overcoat as well and follow me." He took my overcoat from the wardrobe in the corner and tossed it to me. I put it on over my robe.

"Is this really necessary...?" I asked. "I mean, it damn well should be for you to get me out of bed at this hour."

"It is." And with that, he headed to the door of the suite and, quite uncharacteristically for me, I followed him meekly, even sheepishly—I, who had only a few hours earlier, while I drank my wine and ate my supper, pictured

125

myself as the up-and-coming leader in world affairs. There was something in his demeanor, though, that didn't invite refusal. Not a sense of urgency, certainly, but a sense of command based on something sound and reasonable, though as yet undisclosed.

Curfew had been called two hours earlier and the vast hall was now as silent as a churchyard. Only enough light shone from the wall lamps to see one's way safely along the corridor. I peered over the railing of this odd indoor loggia as I followed Vic and saw that all the lights in the great room below, save one large standing lamp, had been extinguished. We made our way quietly, surreptitiously, without words and nearly on tiptoe, to the elevator, the doors of which stood open and waiting, its interior's light streaming out into the darkness of the corridor. Vic entered and I followed, and at a touch of his finger the lift began its descent to the enormous, vaulted basement below.

The silence was getting to me, so I ventured to ask Vic a question that had occurred to me during my conversation with Brother Antoine. "Does Cardinal Fieropasto ever say Mass? I mean, given his…"

"Identity?" said Vic.

"Yes. His identity. It seems strange to me that he would."

"Well, in fact, he doesn't," replied Vic.

"Really? How can he—being a cardinal—not say Mass? Wouldn't that be something of a scandal?"

The elevator came to a stop with a jolt. "Here we are," said Vic, as the doors slid open. We stepped out into the dimly lit interior of the vast, vaulted underworld.

Pausing as the elevator's doors closed behind us, Vic turned to me and said: "He doesn't say Mass for a very simple reason. He's never been ordained. He's always been a lay cardinal."

"I didn't know there was such a thing," I said.

"It was more common in former times," said Vic, gesturing for me to follow him past the refectory entrance and toward another door just visible in the shadows beneath the muted radiance of an amber lamp. "He doesn't receive Communion, either," he continued. "He never has. I'm one of the few people who know about it. He's successfully concealed it from nearly everybody for ages. He has strong mental powers, as you know."

"How is it you know, but others don't?"

"Here's the door to his sleeping quarters," said Vic, ignoring my last question. He withdrew from under his robes a slender key—if "key" is the right word; it looked more like a small wand, the length of an index finger, and it fairly glimmered in the gloom. "Come in. But don't touch anything." And we stepped over the threshold into the blackness. Vic shut the door behind us and, stepping over to a lamp, switched it on.

Here before us was the frugally appointed room Brother Antoine had described to me earlier. It was devoid of artwork, and a single canopied bed, looking like it had come straight from a movie set in Tudor times, adorned with red velvet drapes and faded golden tassels, stood squarely in the center. A side table was next to it, and on it the lamp that Vic had just switched on. There were also a straight-backed chair and a roll-top desk, but not another stick of furniture. There was, however, another door, directly across from the one we had entered, on the other side of the bed, and only partially visible to us. Vic led me toward it.

"We'll go in this way," said Vic. "What you have to see is through here." He inserted the wand-key into the door's lock, unlatched the thumb-grip on the handle, and opened it.

I already knew, from Brother Antoine, what would await us on the other side of that portal: Cardinal Fieropasto's personal laboratory and museum complex. Excitement took hold of me, but also a sense of foreboding—as if what was inside wasn't meant to be interfered with, that we were transgressing some prohibition and invading territory not intended for anyone else's eyes but Fieropasto's.

The interior was dimly lit in a soft amber-colored glow, and so dim was the lighting that it was difficult to see at all. As I stood there in the doorway, Vic moved off and out of sight to our left somewhere. I could hear him moving about some feet away, and I saw the tiny glow of his wand-key for an instant. There was a clanging, clanking sound, as if a metal door had been thrown open (which, in fact, was the case), and within moments the lights—klieg lights from the looks of them—flashed on from high overhead. Vic shut the door of the metal box that had been affixed to the stone wall, from which cables, clamped to the wall by copper bands, could be seen running up towards the vaulted ceiling many feet above us—the controls to the lighting. As if he could read my thoughts, Vic said:

"I've put all the lights on and turned them up full. Now you'll be able to see it all."

XXI

AND then my nose caught in the air the odor that Brother Antoine had described as being like urine and ammonia. It wasn't strong—not yet, at any rate—but it was unpleasant. It seemed to waft up towards us from somewhere in the distance ahead of us. Vic must have noted the look of revulsion on my face. He extracted from the folds of his robes a large handkerchief that was redolent with the scent of oranges, and, handing it to me, said, "Put this over your nose and mouth if the stench in this place gets to you."

"What is it?" I asked. I meant the odor in the atmosphere, but Vic evidently took my question to refer to the place where we were.

"Fieropasto's workshop," he said. "Look." And he gestured to the great expanse before us.

I can only compare the enormous, high-vaulted space of the gallery to the interior of a large city museum. It reminded me in its height and breadth of the Smithsonian or the Metropolitan or the Field Museum in Chicago, only— truth be told—it was much larger and grander than all of them. It extended so far in front of us that its far end was not visible to our sight. And, like those institutions I mentioned, it was also a museum. Upright glass display cases, like those used to exhibit suits of armor, for example, or native artifacts or taxidermied animals, lined the walls on either side of us, lit up brightly from within as well as from without. And great, freestanding glass cases stood before us in the midst of the area, as well. And all this stretched ahead of us for as far as the eye could see.

"Follow me," said Vic, motioning with his finger. He

began to cross the hundred or more feet between us and where the nearest freestanding case stood. I followed him without a word, although I was feeling self-conscious about being in this place clothed only in my pajamas, robe, and overcoat. I had the unaccountable sensation, despite being amply covered from shoulders to toes, which one gets in a dream in which the dreamer is stark naked in a public place.

As we drew closer to the nearest display case I became more and more appalled at what I was viewing within it. When we eventually stopped and stood directly before it, I took in the full horror of its contents. Inside the case a yellow-clad man was seated, or, rather, slumped in an armchair, motionless like a broken doll. It was obvious that the man was long dead and had, in some fashion, been mummified. His features were flat and sunken and blackened, like a partially rotten potato, with a few strands of dark hair combed straight back. He was dressed in the uniform of the house's patients. He held in his stiff, parchment-colored fingers a withered and wrinkled children's book. He had been "arranged" to look, it seemed to me, as if he were reading a bedtime story, perhaps to invisible children. A small brass plaque was bolted to the case in front, and I could see that it explained, in Latin, Greek, German, and English, who this man had been.

"Good Lord," I said with a gasp of instant recognition. "I remember him from my childhood. I watched his program on TV."

He had, in fact, been a popular television personality in America. He had had a program with small children. He would read stories to them and get them to say "funny" things—"cute" things—to entertain the families that tuned him in every Saturday night. Then, suddenly, the news had been that he had gone into early retirement. It was due to medical complications, we had been told, and he needed to be institutionalized. His wife had divorced him not long after that, and, apart from that sad item of news, he had disappeared from the public eye. He had been in his early fifties at the time. So, I surmised, he must have been brought here as a patient, and that told me more than enough; and now here he was, a mummy in a display case in Cardinal Fieropasto's underground museum. I was dumbstruck by the realization.

"He was a bastard," said Vic simply. "Be glad you didn't know him personally when you were a boy. You might have been scarred for life. Now, look around you and see the other cases in this hall. Don't take too long. Just see what surrounds you and remember it. We have other areas to visit before we leave this complex tonight."

I did as he instructed me. Turning this way and that and moving about in a tight circle, making sure I didn't stray too far from him, I took in for as far as I could see them the other cases that stretched away before us into the distance. Every case contained yellow-clad, mummified cadavers. Each body had been distinctively positioned and posed, as had the first, with various, apparently telltale objects in their hands. All were identified as well by brass plaques inscribed in the same four languages. I realized that there must be hundreds of these human remains on display, perhaps even thousands— the great hall looked endless from where we stood. It went on, row upon row, corpse after corpse, until the cases became indiscernible lines to my eyes, eaten up by the incalculable distance.

"What in God's name…?" I breathed.

"They're a sort of butterfly collection, you could say," said Vic, "Fieropasto's hobby—or one of his hobbies. Like the orchids in the greenhouse. To him, this is not all that different from mere taxidermy. It's related to his experiments, his study of the human race. All the patients in this place eventually end up here. When a patient dies, all the people upstairs hear is that he was buried—with all the rites—in the crypt below. That's all anyone knows and nobody ever pursues it further. And, frankly, nobody cares."

"But… but why?" I said. "What's the point of it? He must have a reason—otherwise, why?"

"Why? I suppose the short answer is that he's fascinated by the human capacity to harm its own species, its own environment, and—most of all—the human tendency to degrade the innocent. These *patients*"—Vic emphasized the word with disgust in his voice—"interest him in particular. They're all corrupters and abusers. Some of them were famous in their time. You might be shaken if you saw some of the names on the plaques here—you might be disillusioned. And they've all been susceptible to his suggestions, his whispers in their ears. He planted the seeds, the *thoughts*, to see what would grow in their minds—even in those with impressive brains and influential positions. In fact, every one of them at one time or another possessed some sort of power. But they were so easy to bend, so weak…"

"And he *experimented* on them?" I asked. I was beginning to feel shaky at this point. "How?"

"Psychologically, mostly," replied Vic. "Through suggestion, as I said. The classical term, of course, is 'temptation.' He has also experimented—experiments, I should say, because he hasn't ceased—on their bodies in this place. Castrations, lobotomies, narcotics, *et cetera*—trying always to understand what makes them so unstable. And finally, there's his leisurely pursuit of putting them on display down here, after he's squeezed them dry and used them up. Call them mementos. But, you see, the one thing he *can't* understand—although it intrigues him—is the *mechanism*, as he calls it, of lust or concupiscence, of the human tendency to lack self-control even over the very worst desires. He likes to dig down deep inside his subjects' minds, where the primitive and unconscionable lurk in the shadows of the soul, and sort of tickle these up to the surface. He's an 'angel,' remember—although that term is an accommodation to human ideas. He's not like you. He's not human. Don't try to understand him by human standards."

Vic sighed and looked thoughtful for a moment as I struggled to take in everything he was telling me. Then in a more wistful tone of voice he continued: "People have said a lot of baloney about the devil. He gets depicted as a satyr, of all things, with virile loins, goatish, lustful, that sort of thing. As if *sex* were something that could appeal to him. In fact, he finds it completely repulsive. To him there's nothing more ridiculous than a self-styled, sexually promiscuous 'Satanist.' He's nothing if not a positivist. That reminds me—Aleister Crowley's remains are in here somewhere. He was never actually cremated, you know. Fieropasto arranged some private deal, and he's on display down here in a clown's costume and a pointy hat. The only one not in a yellow uniform, as it happens. Anyway," and Vic allowed a sardonic smile to pass over his lips as he said it, "Fieropasto is a thoroughly bloodless scientist—you might even call him 'Pavlovian,' although it would be more accurate to call Pavlov a 'Fieropastian.' He's more of a Mengele than a Crowley."

"Maybe we should get out of here—I've seen it now," I said, revulsion filling my mind like a fog. I clamped the scented handkerchief Vic had given me over my nose and mouth.

"No," said Vic. "Not yet. We're nowhere near done yet. It's my responsibility to show you all you need to see. You shouldn't leave here with any illusions. Especially about yourself."

These were ominous words, and Vic's hawk-like features somberly looking down at me as he said them were not in the least comforting.

XXII

WE moved on, past case after case of carefully arranged and labeled corpses. The stench of the place, I noted, increased as we proceeded, and I clasped Vic's handkerchief to my face to get as much relief from it as I could. After walking on in silence for what seemed a mile or more, Vic motioned for me to look ahead and off to our right.

"On the other side of that display," he said, "we'll make a turn into the south wing."

Straight ahead of us the hall and the cases appeared to continue on endlessly—there was no end in view. The number of cadavers there, all told, must have been staggering. I looked behind us and saw how great a distance we had already come. The first freestanding case we had encountered was now invisible to us from where we were, and the door through which we had entered the hall was a mere speck beyond that point, just barely detectable to my sight at all.

"Here we are," announced Vic, and we veered to the right and entered another chamber of the underground complex. This one was not quite so overwhelming in size as the main hall, but, even so, it was of tremendous dimensions.

There were no taxidermied bodies on display here. Instead, what these cases contained were thousands of pictures—paintings, lithographs, sketches, photographs—all of them depicting ages upon ages of unimaginable human cruelty, gathered from every race and culture. If the mummies in the grand hall had dismayed me, the cumulative effect of the collection housed in this room was in some regards more shocking. Each image was labeled in Latin, Greek, German, and English, just as the mummies had been, on brass plaques. And, once again, the cases were arranged in neat rows.

I cannot sufficiently describe the horrors I saw there. It would defy my powers of description to provide the horrific and foul particulars of any of them and to express the impact they had on me; but, even if I could describe any of them effectively, I wouldn't wish to do so. I can only tell you that the images—and they were countless—were of every conceivable perversity imaginable. No form of cruelty, torture, violence, sexual abuse, mass murder, degradation, starvation, mutilation, be it in time of war or of peace, in the streets or the prison camp or the bedroom, was excluded. The elderly and infirm stripped of dignity, men and women engaged in acts of unspeakable crudity and defilement, cruelty to animals that beggared the most vicious imagination, the extermination of "undesirables," ethnic cleansings, abortions, mental patients lobotomized, a forest of human beings impaled... seemingly endless atrocities in every direction I looked. I tried to shield my eyes, looking up and away.

"Keep looking," said Vic in a commanding tone. "This is a museum. It's what Cardinal Fieropasto *muses* on."

"I can't... I can't understand any of this," I said. "I mean I can't understand *him*. What is he playing at down here?" My head was swimming. I reached out and steadied myself against the glass of a display case. I've never been squeamish, but now I thought I might faint. "I mean, Fieropasto—was he ever really a pure spirit?"

"Spirit, yes," replied Vic. "But 'pure'?" Then, pointing to a different case, he said, "Take a look there."

Another wave of dizziness passed over me, but I turned again to look where he was pointing and saw he was indicating a set of photographs taken at the Auschwitz concentration camp. I thought I had seen countless photographic treatments of that camp in my time, but these I had never seen before. Vic, I saw, was now pointing out one photograph in particular. I bent closer to the one he indicated and what I saw in it, quite distinctly, were the features of Fieropasto. He looked no younger than he did at the present day. And that wasn't all. In the photo, he was standing beside someone whose features I instantly recognized. The man in the picture was, without question, Josef Mengele. The two of them—Fieropasto and Mengele—were staring down coldly at the nude bodies of a row of starving Jewish boys. These children were lined up in a stance like that of military attention before the two men. Chills shot through me as I looked at the photograph and the hairs on the nape of my neck tingled as if in reaction to an electric shock, and, for the first time in that miserable place, tears came into my eyes.

"More like Mengele... You said he was more like Mengele..." My voice trailed off.

Vic said nothing. He stood glowering, but not at me. He merely raised his right arm and pointed a long index finger to yet another case that stood directly behind me. I slowly turned around, fearful of what new horror I would see, and what met my gaze surpassed my fear. What I saw brought the bile into my mouth.

There was image after image of the defilement, torture, and destruction of children, horrid and brutal, refined and savage, all preserved under glass and labeled as if by some pitiless, objective, clinical researcher—Fieropasto, no doubt. And now my tears flowed and I broke down and sobbed. Unable to continue without a moment's respite, I turned my eyes upwards and saw above the case the Cardinal's coat-of-arms. I recalled the anecdote of how its design had originated in a jest—and I realized now that the meaning of that "comic" image had really been no jest to him at all. The mocking man-faced snake in the tree above the two sad apes, beguiling the creatures below him, baiting them and cursing them—*that* was Fieropasto looking down on humanity, even on the smallest child.

I swore under my breath.

"There's a stairway we'll need to take to get to the lower level," said Vic, still not looking in my direction. "Let's move on."

"The level below?" I repeated. "There's more? Haven't we seen enough already?"

"There's more to see."

"Why have you brought me down here?" I said. "Was it to prove to me that Fieropasto really is the devil—that he's really evil? But there's something I don't get at all—aren't *you* in league with him?"

"Aren't *you*?" he retorted, turning his hawk-like gaze toward me. "Just an hour ago you were all jacked up to go conspire with him. He made you a few promises, and you were ready to go right along. Isn't that right? And I bet you'd still take the carrot he's offering you."

"Now hold on—why do you say that?" I was shocked by his seeming ability to read my mind. Inside, I knew he was right. "Look, all right—yes, I was flattered by him. I admit it. And, damn it, you're right, I'd still take that power he's offering me. But I'd do it only to thwart him now. I wouldn't take it for any other reason."

"So, you think you're just going to take that power from him and then turn around and kick him in the ass with it? You honestly think that's going to happen?" He smiled scornfully and shook his head. "He has some years on you, buddy."

"Yes, I know I could do it," I said defensively. "I'm not a neophyte. I know how to handle bad guys and beat them at their own game, too. You're forgetting I've got years of experience in business and politics. For Christ's sake, I've broken whole regimes."

"Watch your mouth," said Vic. "I doubt you know what 'for Christ's sake' means."

This response flustered me.

"So now you're going to play priest with me," I said angrily. "About time, too, I guess. Look, I'm telling you straight. As soon as I get half a chance, Fieropasto is going to be my first item of business. Somebody has to take him on. I'm going to crush him. I'm going to destroy him... destroy him... I'm going to destroy him and all his works... I'll... I'll..."

But I couldn't go on. Something inside me—something like panic and nausea combined—made me stop, and I leaned my head dizzily against the glass.

"Yeah, yeah," said Vic. He turned away from me and headed in the direction of the far end of the wing. "Now let's get going," he said over his shoulder, without pausing in his stride. "We've got a stairway to descend."

I followed him dazedly to the far end of the wing, where we turned to our left. There was a small entrance in the wall, which proved to be a short passageway. Vic entered and I trailed behind him. Not far inside it we came to a narrow, twisting, descending stairway, the steps of which were of well worn, evidently ancient stones. Down it we went, spiraling on and on, always to the left. In my imagination I conceived of it as a sort of stone serpent, coiled and rearing itself upright on its tail far below, and us going down to its very tip by way of the creature's innards. And as we went, that dreadful odor like ammonia and urine grew stronger, to the point that I could scarcely breathe without gagging.

At the end of our descent there was an ochre-colored metal door, shut, and rather nondescript, like a door one might see in a laboratory or medical institute. Vic motioned to me to pause, while he extracted again his shining wand-key. He inserted it in the keyhole and I heard the lock release, and with a push of Vic's hand the door swung open.

Now I saw before us a brightly lit and sizable room. In appearance it was like an operating theater or the sort of room I had seen in modern funeral homes in the United States in which bodies were embalmed or cremated. Cabinets and counters of cold aluminum lined the theater, and there were four or five tables of the same material visible as well. Bottles of various liquids, cotton swabs, hypodermic needles in plastic containers, and an array of whirring and clicking electrical equipment and monitors met my eyes.

We went in. The room was icy, like a meat locker, and I drew the collar of my overcoat up around my ears for warmth. Vic pointed silently to our right. I looked and gasped, and held the handkerchief even tighter to my face. What I saw, splayed out on a cold aluminum table some fifteen feet away, was the naked bluish-gray body of a man, obviously quite dead. The cadaver was swollen and bulbous, but with long skinny legs. It looked waxy, cold, and froglike. Vic went over to it and, motioning me to join him, we stood there side by side looking down on the stiff, cold features of Mr. Charlie.

XXIII

"JUST get him prepared. Downstairs," Fieropasto had said to the nurse as Mr. Charlie had been escorted away the night before. A disturbing notion now dawned in my mind of what "getting him prepared" had meant.

I saw that an incision had been made, then stitched up again, which ran from the middle of Mr. Charlie's chest clear down to just above the genitals. Beside the aluminum table on which the corpse lay, there stood a mobile medical trolley. On it there were six sealed clear glass jars in which human internal organs could be descried, submerged in a somewhat cloudy liquid. A seventh, smaller jar contained two blue eyes, and next to that jar—ready, apparently, to replace the two fleshy ones afloat in the smaller jar—were two blue glass eyes. I backed off and looked away, feeling nauseous.

"It looks like," said Vic without emotion, "Mr. Charlie is almost ready for exhibition."

"How did he die?" I managed to say between gasps for air.

Vic didn't reply, but simply stared impassively at me.

"He used to be an important man in the Church," I said after an awkward pause. "I remembered who he was earlier today and..." I broke off, not knowing what to say after that.

"A reminder that vestments don't make the man," said Vic dispassionately.

Vic's lack of feeling vexed me, and something in me flared up again. "Well," I said with uncontrolled agitation in my voice, "you're something of a pretender yourself, aren't you?"

"No. I'm not a pretender," replied Vic, unfazed. "Not the way you mean it and certainly not in the way Charlie here was. I know exactly what I am. But the big question tonight, Mr. President, is: Do you know what *you* are?"

Again his intense gaze seemed to penetrate me.

I was still feeling giddy and nauseous. The coldness of the room and its atrocious stench were getting to me. Vic meanwhile seemed oblivious to both.

"Can we move along?" I said.

"Yeah, okay." Vic then pointed to a second entrance, directly across the theater from the one through which we had entered. "That way," he said. "There's one more thing you've got to see."

I grimaced, nodded, and followed his lead. We exited the icy theater through the other doorway. We had now entered a dismally lighted corridor of yellowish marble, which reminded me of nothing so much as a passageway in a mortuary I had visited years ago.

"It all seems like a dream to me," I said, making a half-hearted attempt at something approximating normal conversation.

"Oh, yeah?" asked Vic.

"A dream seems like real life while you're dreaming it," I said. "You never know what's coming next, just like in real life. It's not like reading a book. With a book you can flip to the back and see how it ends. But a dream just meanders in a pointless way, and everything is unexpected—like it is in real life. Then, again, my dreams really don't seem pointless to me. They seem to have a meaning. Especially lately."

"I never dream," said Vic.

At the end of the passageway, which wasn't very long, I could see another door. I went on talking to stave off the growing apprehension and dread I felt as we came closer to it. The odor was receding a little now, thank God, the further we went from the theater with its cadaver behind us.

"If the brain authors the dream," I babbled stupidly on while we advanced, "why is it, if it's me whose mind is constructing the dream, why is the dream more like real life and not more like a story I'm making up? Why don't I know

141

what's coming next in my own dream if the dream is the product of my own brain?" I suddenly realized I was sounding stoned.

"Sober yourself up," said Vic. "We're here."

We were standing before the door. It was a heavy door, constructed of wood and very dark, with iron hinges and an iron bolt, and its appearance reminded me of the entrance to a Gothic church. Vic once again inserted his wand-key into the lock, and the door slowly, creakingly swung inwards. We stepped in, and there before us was another room lined with bright display cases. As before, each case was filled with photographs faultlessly mounted and labeled, and also objects—many of them I recognized instantly as related to my own life. In fact, I realized with a jolt that there was an overwhelming number of items I recognized and also that the room was spacious. I began to feel a new and unexpected sense of discomfort. I don't mean that I felt physically uneasy—although I did—but *psychologically* uneasy, and I was reluctant to look more closely at the objects and photographs. I knew that this space *was all about myself*; that everything in it pertained to *my life*, to my biography.

"This room," said Vic, drawn up to his full height and overshadowing me, looking more imposingly raptor-like than ever, "means more to Fieropasto than anything else down here. It's dedicated to the one person he's pinned all his cherished hopes on, the one person, besides himself, he can really be said to love. Maybe after tonight you thought Fieropasto couldn't love anybody, but you'd be wrong. There's one person he's always thought of as his very own, precious adopted son, in whom he's very touchingly well-pleased. What you're about to see, Mr. President, you can call his keepsakes, his special album of favorite baby pictures. So, Mr. President, get ready, brace yourself—*this is your life!*"

And I heard what sounded suspiciously like Vic repressing a laugh.

XXIV

WHAT I felt as I stood in that hall of memories—*my own memories* collected and displayed by one I had begun to loathe—defy any powers I have for description. Even now, feeling them again as I write this, I can't find adequate words to express them. The best I can manage is to say that I experienced something like humiliation, fury, violation, and sadness all mingled and intertwined within me—and also, I'm ashamed to say, an unbidden sense of exaltation.

Physically, I was dizzy and hadn't yet recovered from the ammoniac odor. I had also been left emotionally shattered by the contents of the museum above and the lab with its splayed froglike human cadaver. And now—there was *this*. What sense could be made of it? What sense could be made of any of it? Or of Vic bringing me here in the first place? And whom did Vic represent? Was he, as he had indicated to me, loyal to me? Or was he Fieropasto's instrument? Or—and the thought suddenly crossed my mind—was he the agent of a third party as yet undisclosed? He had shape-shifted so many times now—barber, security chief, cardinal at the Vatican, and now my personal Virgil or Ghost of Christmas Present—that I could no longer even begin to guess what his *true* role could be.

I swallowed as best I could my unease and biliousness and began to study more closely our surroundings. All about us were photographs and even items—for example, a pacifier, a battered tricycle that had once belonged to me as a child, a wind-up Jack-in-the-Box, a colorful mobile of plastic birds that once hung above my crib, sets of toy soldiers I had collected, items of boyhood clothing, a Daniel Boone TV-program-themed lunchbox, and other childhood articles. In another case were post-adolescent items—a college ring of mine (long gone missing), a fountain pen with my initials on it, a large printed sign with the acronym SNARC on it, dated from early in the company's history, and many other such half-forgotten or long-lost objects. My whole life to date was represented all about us.

And there were photographs, blown up and mounted, of my parents and grandparents, of my first Christmas, of me holding my teddy bear, of our family's dogs and cats... And here was my younger brother, who had died in a skiing accident at the age of nineteen. Grade school class photos, my high school graduation, the universities I had attended, the jobs I had worked to get myself through college, my few brief years in the Air Force (which had taken me to New Mexico in the first place), my wedding to Catherine in Alamogordo, the beginnings of my business in Albuquerque, my public career afterward—all documented scrupulously, carefully, even delicately. There was picture after picture of Catherine and me together, many of them intimate, exhibiting shared happiness at first, and then more and more an emotional distancing began to creep into them, then sorrow, tension, conflict, and finally separation... our faces growing bitter, frowning faces, faces creased by internal suffering, our hair gone prematurely gray. It was all there. The camera (*who*, I wondered had been behind the camera?) didn't lie. We had been childless. And there it was, evident in the pictures: the pain, the tears, and those moments of mutual recrimination. And then, of course, there was the pictorial chronicle of my career: how intrusive that career looked here, how time-consuming and time-wasting, robbing us of so much; there in those pictures, unmistakably visible to me, were my self-importance and inexhaustible self-promotion, my position in the world ever on the rise, ever mounting high and higher, and the smugness showing ever more plainly on my face with every passing year; the busyness, the excuses, the pushing aside of everything and everyone else—including Catherine—for the sake of the business, later for the sake of international responsibilities, and finally for the sake of politics, but most of all for the sake of *me*. How insufferable I appeared to myself here. For the first time in my life, I could see plainly how insupportable my self-importance must have seemed for everyone around me who had put up with my "successes." Picture after picture after picture told the ugly truth of it. The camera (*who had taken these pictures?*) didn't lie.

And as I looked I found myself growing sicker and sicker of *me*. Who really *was* this constructed person—this avatar, this mountebank, this deceiver, phony, and fraud? Whose was this well-groomed head (groomed, in fact, by Vic more often than not)? Whose were these self-conscious, self-loving, self-adoring celebrity features, smiling falsely, smiling to please the cameras and the crowds, so pompous, so foolish, and so fake...? Who had I been kidding all these years? Myself? The people? Yes, the people, mostly—all those people, cheering me on, hanging on my every word. Even my most inane and trite utterances had been treated as sage pronouncements. And how I had played on the gullibility of my supporters and sycophants! I had been shameless. It was all there, all visible, all sickening. They had been duped so easily, believing I was the anointed bringer of change...

And the longer I gazed on those photographs—and I lost all sense of time as I did so, though it couldn't have been for long—of throngs lauding me and hailing me and virtually worshiping me, the more unnerved and frightened I felt myself becoming. Image after image of myself began to wear on me, to weigh me down, to rub me the wrong way, to rub my nose in the dirt—my own self-made dirt. I had not only been the object of adulation by others; I had been the object of adulation by *me*. But what *they* hadn't known, though I had known it all too well, was that the personal image I had projected was bogus and hollow. It looked pretty damned good, it sold copy; but it wasn't real. All the while I had been climbing, I had also been bullying, manipulating, lying—or at least bending the truth—and ever posing for the media. And it had always worked in my favor, and these pictures showed I knew it worked and gloried in it and couldn't be satiated and wanted more. I always wanted more. I was always unsatisfied and, it hit me now, unsatisfiable.

And whoever had taken these pictures had mirrored not only events, they had captured my soul as well—the ugliness under the exterior seemed to me to shadow its way out through the very pores of my photogenic skin and the fabric of my stylish clothes. Every image of my glamorous, smiling countenance looked like a death's head in this place, a clown's face, a mask fixed more and more firmly in place as the years unrolled, covering up nothing much underneath. It dawned on me in that deeply buried realm that stank of corruption and corpses and embalming—and the growing recognition revolted me—how like Fieropasto I actually was. I really didn't know who I was.

"As I said, if there's one thing in this world Fieropasto feels anything like affection for," said Vic, "it's you. Your career, all your achievements—even those achievements you never even witnessed or cared to know about—even those he's carefully documented and displayed here. You should feel honored that you've had such a doting patron, such a second father. But, now here's something—you've got to come over here and take a good look at these."

He was on the other side of the room, looking not at me, but at a row of display cases there. "Here are some achievements of yours that the Cardinal's highlighted with special care. They say a lot about the sort of leader you've been in the past. They show so much promise of the leader you'll undoubtedly be in the future. I guarantee you've never looked at them before—like so many of your most lasting accomplishments. Look, see how they've affected so many lives."

Hesitantly, dragging my feet a bit, I came over to his side and looked at the photographs he had indicated. I froze upon seeing them and simply stood aghast. Here were the images of smoking homes in the Middle East. In one expanded, beautifully mounted photo I saw a woman in tattered clothes, bloodied and kneeling beside what appeared to be the ripped and wrenched body of a child, screaming out her lamentations into the black smoke overhead. In another I saw the charred corpse of a man who had been burned alive in the wreckage of a white van, his features smashed in like a rotten pumpkin. There were scores of such scenes. Buildings reduced to rubble, children dismembered and crushed, women mangled and men torn apart, the corpses of livestock and pets, body parts strewn about like branches after a windstorm, people in flames, cars in flames, homes in flames, burning streets, burning mosques, burning churches. I knew what these pictures revealed. These were the collateral results of "regime changes" and "kinetic actions" unleashed at my say-so, the aftermath of drone attacks I had ordered, the consequences of missiles launched and bombs dropped, of military operations that had become orgies of mass murder, mutilation, rape, and other cruelties. And these had often been pitilessly inflicted with the advanced technologies my own company had invented—which had, in turn, made me a very rich man and had propelled me into the public limelight of adulation.

"The free world protecting its freedoms," said Vic. "Isn't that what you folks like to tell yourselves? Most of these folks never had many freedoms themselves, and they sure never had any time on their hands or wish to attack yours. But, what the hell...? People die. Sometimes, lots. There's always going to be collateral, too, whatever that means. I guess the best we can do is just do it cleanly, hygienically, at a safe distance, where everything is just a few gray streaks on a monitor, and get it over with. But it's not all bad news, is it? Other people are safe, some of them very safe. And some of them thrive. You can make a lot of money in your racket, get a lot of humanitarian credit, lots of kudos, and lots of votes if you say you'll keep the refugees out after you bomb their homes. Migrants, I guess you'd call them, or caravans—now, there's a good word. It makes you see camels and wandering, shifty-looking pickpockets and tattooed gang members and sex traffickers and druggies—you get the idea. Yeah, 'caravans' is a swell word. And then there are the infrastructures of the places you liberated from whatever you liberated them from. Everybody benefited from that devastation, I guess. Not just the billionaires, whose pockets you were lining."

I could only groan in reply. But he went on:

"Well, you had a good run—haven't you, Mr. President? And now you've got the chance to do it all over again on a worldwide scale. These pictures are here because Fieropasto so admires the firmness you demonstrated in the past. He approves of your toughness and resolution. He blesses every bomb, every particle of white phosphorous. And he loves you very much. You're exactly what he wants for this world. Someone who can destroy things confidently, in the conviction that you're right. A man after the devil's heart—the very child of his heart."

"But I was trying to put an end to the violence, the terrorism," I moaned, clutching my gut. "I succeeded in that. Not perfectly, okay, I admit it, but I protected lots and lots of people."

"You protected every bureaucracy," said Vic, turning on me with such sudden ferocity that I reeled backwards on my heels, "every hierarchy, every political system, every commercial interest, every billionaire with deadly force." He pointed to another display case nearby. "And come over here! Here are those caravans you protected the richer nations of the West from. Looks like a few waterlogged bodies there—you certainly worked wonders. Don't be afraid—look at them. Don't you want to see the mark you've made on the world? And over here"—he swung around to yet another case—"the detention camps you kept running. Dangerous children in icebox conditions, separated from their parents, some of them dying, some of them getting lost forever... Lousy bookkeeping, I guess, but nothing's perfect. Oh, and here are the other camps you kept for the detained—I suppose you could say some of these pictures are of what you might call 'enhanced interrogation techniques.' Not for the squeamish, but you can handle it. Did those techniques work? Well, what does it matter? They made a point. Somebody had to make a point. Somebody had to be man enough to do the right thing. Luckily, there was always you, Mr. President, Mr. Secretary, Mr. Cardinal's Man, Mr. Antichrist. You've always been the man. Your accomplishments—and there are loads of them, I got to tell you—really speak for themselves. You'll be judged on their merits. Oh, not just the ones in the glossy photos, the pictures of cheering crowds and glamorous smiles and grand events held in your honor. For every picture like that, there are dozens more showing these, your true achievements—the dead, the dismembered, the downtrodden, the fleeing, the tortured, the raped, the burned and charred..."

But I could hear nothing more of what he was saying. I was openly sobbing by this time, and repeating over and over, "God damn me, God damn me, God damn me..."

Then, utterly drained of what remained of my strength and willpower, I collapsed on my knees and vomited. I pitched forward and sank down, babbling to Vic through choking, gagging moans—it was finally, crushingly all too much for me. I lay there, crumpled, half-conscious, my face pressed against the cold marble floor.

And then I could hear voices above me—men's voices—

and the sounds of booted feet. I managed to turn my head a bit and glance blearily upwards, and I saw the figures of Vic's men in SWAT gear bending over me.

"Oh, God," I mumbled. "Not you again."

"Get him out of here," I heard Vic say to them.

Strong hands grabbed hold of my arms and legs and lifted me up onto some sort of carrier—a stretcher, perhaps. I couldn't see it, I didn't care—all I wanted was to get out, get away, or maybe—the thought passed through my mind—just die.

And then I blacked out.

XXV

THE blackness took on shapes, and the shapes became a vision.

I was alone in an automobile, seated behind the steering wheel, in a long line of stalled traffic. The engine was purring, but the car was going nowhere. The queue of motionless vehicles was bumper to bumper, all facing downhill on an icy, steep mountain road. Dark evergreens towered overhead on either side of the road and seemed even blacker than the enveloping, starless night. Snow was falling hard, and the wipers periodically brushed the alighting flakes from the windshield. I could make out that all these stationary cars were black in color, but their occupants weren't visible to me through the blizzard. None of the vehicles had their headlights switched on.

Far ahead, at the bottom of the slope we were on, I could discern the flashing blue and red lights of police cars. I surmised that a crisis of some sort, an accident perhaps, had caused the traffic on the mountain to come to a halt. The emergency lights flashing below seemed somehow sinister to me. There were no sounds other than those of the snow's barely noticeable alighting and the regular sweeping of the windshield wipers. We sat as immobile as stone, the time passing at a rate of what seemed an hour per minute. I was growing steadily more impatient and agitated.

As my anxiety mounted, the thought of reversing the automobile and backtracking to a side road entered my mind. Somehow I knew there was a side road nearby, one I could reach with a little luck. How I could have known that, I don't know; nothing about that road was in the least familiar to me. But I determined that I would take that side route and get off the mountain that way. With that decided, I quickly threw the vehicle into reverse—only to realize that there were also cars lined up behind me, all of them black, with unlit headlights. Looking in my rear-view mirror I saw, with alarm, that the windshields of all those automobiles behind me were dark blanks—I couldn't see into them. The vehicles looked, in fact, completely empty. No occupants were visible inside them, as if these cars had been abandoned with their engines running, their exhaust issuing like an acrid mist about them.

I jammed on the brakes, so as not to collide with the car directly in back of me, and this foolish action caused my car to spin wildly to my right on the ice. I had succeeded only in swinging the vehicle around sideways, and my front wheels were now stuck in a narrow ditch on the side of the road, the car's rear pointing upwards. I found myself facing the trees and a row of white guard posts, unable to go backwards or forwards. No matter how much I gunned the engine and the wheels spun, kicking up snow and mud, I couldn't manage to get the car out of that ditch.

In frustration, I switched off the ignition and the engine fell silent. I didn't want to try starting it up again, fearing I might drain the battery, but it also meant that the heat inside the car was now off—and it was intensely cold outside. The long line of black vehicles remained motionless, the snow continued cascading from the sky, and the unseen occupants of the cars behind me—assuming there were any at all— could only have been staring mutely at my predicament, since no reaction came from any of them. The red and blue emergency lights continued to flash noiselessly in the distance at the bottom of the incline.

"Damn it all," I heard myself saying. "What am I doing here? How in hell do I get out of here?"

Panic pressed itself up from my solar plexus and on up my

spine. Up to the nape of my neck. My heart was racing crazily. I had to make some decision, but I didn't know what decision to make. So there I sat, stuck, my car's nose in a rut, its rear end pointing to the skies, catastrophe ahead and something like menace behind. I had no way to go forward and no way to go back. With the engine off, the cold became ever more biting within the car, and eventually, I knew, it would be unendurable.

What to do? My dread and vexation were reaching a point of eruption. I wanted to rant and pound the steering wheel. Instead, I sank into a funk, flattened emotionally, despairing and so mentally wasted I couldn't think lucidly anymore.

"I have to do something," I kept saying to myself. "I have to do something."

And then, from the backseat, a voice responded, startling me. "Mr. President," it said.

It was Vic's voice. I looked up at the rear-view mirror and saw his eyes shining back into mine, the rest of his features obscured in the darkness.

"Get out of the car *now*," he said.

I didn't think, I didn't question him. Despite my befuddlement, I just did what he told me. I got out.

I began stumblingly to trudge out into the snow. Where on earth I was heading I had no idea whatever. I simply kept moving blindly through the snowfall, directionless, mentally numbed, freezing cold. And I kept on going like that until, thoroughly exhausted, I tripped over something large—a stone, a branch, I don't know what—and dropped facedown into the snow. My eyes were shut tight and I didn't want to move. I just lay there in that state for some moments, gasping for breath.

"Come on," said the voice of Vic again, close to my ear. "Get up. You're here."

XXVI

I RAISED my face from the snow and pushed myself up into a crouching position. I was still on the mountain, or at least I can say I was on *a* mountain, but now there was a sky of cloudless azure overhead. I was clear of the woods, out in the open. A lingering whiteness of snow shone among the rocks that were visible here and there, jutting from a carpet of fresh green grass; it was early spring and the sun was shining and warm. It was so warm in fact that I stood up, wobbling unsteadily and blinking my eyes for a few moments there in the bright daylight, and removed the overcoat I was wearing over my robe. I could see that I was on the mountain's summit. Blossoming trees spangled the broad expanse of meadow, as did crocuses, irises, and snowdrops. A soft breeze moved refreshingly, tousling my hair, lifting my spirits, sweetly fragrant with the scents of a reviving earth.

God, I thought, how good it is to be here.

After the horrors I had just quitted so enigmatically, but welcome for all that, I probably should have been amazed; but, no, I felt no such reaction. Instead, I felt consoled by the new surroundings, as if I were precisely where I needed to be, as if I had been expected (by whom, I couldn't have said) to arrive just here and just now. And oddly, too, the surroundings seemed inexplicably familiar to me, as if some memory of them had long lain buried down deep in my mind and, could I just remember hard enough, I might resurrect it. But the memory eluded my efforts to recall it. As foolish or silly as it might seem now with the telling, I felt like I was somehow "at home."

Then I spotted Vic some yards away off to my right, on the

opposite side of a small gushing stream, conspicuous in his red robes in the sunshine against the blue sky, seated nonchalantly on a white rock. When he saw that I noticed him, he smiled at me and then pointed a long finger in the direction of a prominent hillock visible in the distance. It looked to be about half a mile away, and I could see that someone was seated on it and that there was a small fire sending up a spiral of smoke between the feet of that someone.

I walked in his direction and as I drew closer, I saw that he was dressed in coarse wool and wore sandals. He looked like a shepherd and indeed I saw there were sheep roaming nearby, nibbling at the sward. The thought struck me, judging from his attire, that I must have been transported to some locale in the Middle East.

The man had a dark shawl over his head, shading him from the sun's glare, so his features were in shadow. When I reached him, he casually took out of a capacious leather pouch beside him a round loaf of rough bread, broke off a piece, and, handing it to me, he motioned for me to be seated on a flat stone next to him in front of the fire. As I took the bread I couldn't help noticing that his wrists were terribly scarred.

And now his features were visible to me, and they were striking in that they conveyed both toughness and gentleness. His dark face was almost as leathery in its creases as the pouch beside him. His black beard was flecked with gray. The eyes were chestnut and had a concentrated, intense gaze to them that gave me the impression that he comprehended my thoughts. Here was a man who had the general appearance of calm benevolence and yet, it seemed to me, he might be stern as well—even roused to anger. There was some suggestion of "wildness" about him, for lack of a better word, something unconventional and unmanageable. I was apprehensive, but not unnerved by him.

I sat down beside him. I didn't need to ask who he was. I

took a bite of the bread and sat chewing it, staring into the small fire and enjoying the incense of the wood smoke.

After a while he spoke in an easy and unhurried manner, as if we were continuing a conversation we had already begun and were merely resuming it. That he spoke in faultless English seemed entirely natural to me at the time and only later struck me as surprising.

"I was taken to a mountain much like this one once," he said, looking into the fire, "by the person you know as 'Fieropasto.' I was given a vision there of all the kingdoms of the world spread out before me. And a stupendous sight it was. It was one of the unsubtle ways he sought to distract me. Now the kingdoms of the world are spread out before you. What are you going to do about it?"

"I... I suppose," I replied, nonplussed by the question, "I suppose... I mean I think... perhaps, I should shoulder the responsibility... do my duty. It wasn't *your* calling, I know. But, well... it seems to be mine. I think I could shoulder it, but... I suppose I could use some help...?" I trailed off uncertainly, quizzically.

He turned his head and looked directly into my eyes. "Yes. Go on," he said. "And what calling would that be, which you think you could shoulder?"

"Well... I guess I believe I have a calling to take up the task everything in my life prepared me for," I said hesitantly, nervously picking at the piece of bread with my fingers. "But," I added hastily, "I wouldn't do it the way Fieropasto wants. No, I'd step into the office and try, you know, to... to perform my duties according to *your* principles..." I realized my words were lame. I tried to bolster them a bit, but succeeded only in sounding more diffident than if I hadn't bothered. "I know I haven't given your words sufficient thought before... Anyway, I can't very well refuse my vocation entirely... Wouldn't I be burying my talent if I did that, if you don't mind me citing one of your own parables...?"

"Ah, I see," he said, and fell silent.

"I have a responsibility," I began again, filling in that silence, "and it's unavoidable *not* to do what I'm destined to do. I mean... I'm assuming I'm destined for it. It seems—and one of your Dominicans assured me just the other day—that even the Bible puts me in that role. Predestination, I mean. It's what I'm *supposed* to do... Destiny and, well, all that..."

Now that I was seated here on this mountain out in the sunlight, sharing bread with him, everything I was saying sounded utterly idiotic to me. The certainty that had blossomed in me in Fieropasto's surroundings concerning my inevitable future now seemed faraway and vapid, unraveling and dispelled.

"One of *my* Dominicans?" he said, and I thought I noticed the trace of a smile. "You talk of 'destiny,' 'predestination,' and what you're 'supposed' to do. Do you believe this? Have you considered that all your notions might be *wrong*, that perhaps you've been too quick to accept them? That you could, in fact, merely let them go? That you could let the dead bury their dead and you could leave your 'destiny' behind? Have you no decision left to make?"

This was, I admit, a disorienting set of thoughts. He stated it all so starkly that there was no hiding from myself that, even now, after all I had gone through beneath Fieropasto's stronghold, I still secretly coveted the role I had allowed myself to believe was inevitable. All along, I realized, I had desired it should be my destiny. Inexorably predestination entailed a duty that couldn't be shirked. But it was I who willed it so. I had been working hard for it. Always wanting to stand out, to be special, to be seen to carry responsibility on my shoulders with herculean industriousness, seen to exercise great influence, I could picture myself curing the world's ills. That ambition had been inside me long before Fieropasto revealed himself to me. He had only spurred me on. I was face to face with myself now and what I saw, to my abhorrence, was the face of Fieropasto.

"My dear son," it seemed to say. "All the kingdoms of the world are spread out before you. You can have them all. They're yours for the taking. You still can step in and be the savior this unmanageable buffoon beside you failed to be. Don't throw it away."

"You say you're predestined to your role," said the man in rustic woolen garb, eating his peasant bread, smelling of wood smoke, sheep ruminating in the grass nearby. "I'm telling you you're not."

"But," I objected, sounding unsettlingly like a child in Sunday School, "isn't it, you know, 'written' that you won't return in glory unless I—I mean, the Antichrist or whatever it's called—comes to power before that? Isn't that *predestined* to happen?"

"Is it?" he said.

"I… I rather thought it was," I replied in a low voice.

"What I said was that I'm with you always until the end," he said. "I'm right here with you now. And I'm telling you that you have a choice. The end will come for you when it comes, and I will be there when it does."

"But… what of… what of *the Antichrist?*" I said, not really wishing to draw further attention to the title, but needing now to know. "What about '666'?"

"You are full of anxious thoughts," he said, biting off a bit of the bread and chewing it thoughtfully. "You should know that many 'antichrists' have come and gone and I remain. So, you've been offered a crown for a little while. What of it? I was offered one, too. But the only crown I ever wore was made of spikes. All the world's kingdoms will come and go. They always do. Why throw away your life just to gain and hold on to power?"

I looked into the smoldering fire, unable to look him in the eye. "But… but I have worked so long and hard," I stammered, "and… and… the world is such shit. Somebody's got to make things better… Everything… *everything* in my whole life has equipped me for this and there are billions of people who will support me… Couldn't it… couldn't this just possibly be… *God's* will? My destiny…?"

And now the underlying sternness of his character hardened visibly beneath his gentle exterior. I began to feel a sense of dread in the pit of my stomach. He looked to me as if he might actually strike me, and it shook me.

"*God's* will for you," he said with adamancy, "is to go against your 'destiny.' If the Son sets you free, you are free indeed—and I'm setting you free. You don't have to do anything but follow after me, though that will be hard enough. You have no responsibility to rule over anyone, much less the world. You have only one thing to shoulder, one necessary thing to take up, and that will be your cross. Without it you'll never come to your senses. You don't have to fulfill anybody's schemes for your future—not Fieropasto's and not your own. Forget your plans. Free yourself from them and follow me."

"But what about the world?" I said. "Just leave it to its own devices? Just turn my back on its needs?"

He frowned at that, looking exasperated, and I felt more ridiculous than ever. "The world," he said, witheringly, "would be much better off if those persons who believed it was their 'destiny' to command it would leave it alone. If they possessed sincere awareness, they would know that nothing is 'left to its own devices' without their interference, that the sun still rises and sets without them, the rivers still flow, the flowers of the field are still arrayed more gloriously than Solomon, and the birds of the air are still fed without toiling for it. If all the leaders of the nations were to step down from their positions tomorrow and, perhaps, take up raising goats in the mountains, the world could get along without a single one of them. The only truly 'great ones' in the world are those who give themselves to be servants to others and raise up those in greatest need."

I heard the birds singing in the trees as they flitted from branch to flowering branch. I felt the breeze against my cheek and ruffling my hair. In the distance I saw Vic, still seated on a rock, unmoving, like a Buddha in crimson. Deep peace was again settling all around me, and it was mysteriously settling inside me also. Shutting my eyes, I breathed quietly, listening to the crackle of the fire, feeling the sunlight, and as I did so my endlessly noisy and demanding train of thoughts—for the first time in I couldn't remember how long—seemed stilled. There was in everything a strange new tranquility. It began to dawn on me, in that stillness, that, really, honestly, I didn't have a personal worry in the world, and also that the world hadn't a worry that I could relieve by exercising mastery over it. Or, to put it differently, the only way I could in some tiny way alleviate the world's troubles was, first, to alleviate my own, and that meant—and now it hit me with the unexpected force of a religious awakening— my *disappearing* in some sense that I could not yet conceive.

I opened my eyes and looked at the man beside me.

"And Fieropasto? What about him?"

"Ah, the prodigal," he said, poking at the embers with a stick. "He will continue to flee as he has done for ages, 'down the nights and down the days,' right to the very edge of existence. I will let him get so far as almost to be snuffed out like a candle flame, if necessary. And then I will do something that will be my own strange work. I will become the tempter and he the tempted and the roles will be reversed. I will extend to him the possibility of holding on to life and coming back up out of the depths to which he has fled. I'll give him his final chance. Once upon a time, on a mountain like this one, he tempted me with valueless things. But I will tempt him with the fullness of existence itself. The prodigal may finally come home with me. He is, after all, a lost child, a runaway. He's petulant, a liar, and worse, a murderer—in need of great forgiveness and many long ages of purgation. But he might come back in the end. I am drawing all things to myself. Including that prodigal, if he will. You see, there is one, small thing in him which I can lay hold of, one piece of him that undermines all his detachment. It's the hook that might reel him in. Can you guess what it is?"

I was bewildered. "No," I said, "I can't." And I couldn't.

And then he stood up, removing the shawl from his head, and said with a smile, "Why, it's his love for you!"

And he laughed with such good humor that I found myself laughing as well, and I heard Vic laughing, and it seemed as if everything was suddenly shaking like an earthquake. The face before me seemed to radiate with light and fill my vision, growing brighter and brighter until it shone like the sun. The sound of his laughter had changed into a sound like the rumbling of thunder, like the roar of many waters, like Niagara Falls. His figure grew incandescent and I had to shield my watering eyes. I was laughing, but I realized that I was also weeping and shaking in awe—all three simultaneously.

And then, once again, the universe seemed to revolve madly in my head, and the sun swung round me in great arcs, and I heard myself crying out as I toppled backwards into a free-fall, tossing and flailing head over heels into the dark vacuum of unconsciousness.

XXVII

I WOKE up in a bed.

At first I could remember nothing of the things I had seen or the places I had been the past few days. I groggily supposed I was still in my apartment in New York. But then, very gradually, I emerged from my mental fog into greater and greater clarity, and memories of Vic, my abduction, Fieropasto, the horrors of the underground museum, and then—had it been a vision?—those final, dumbfounding moments on the mountain came flooding back into my mind. I opened my eyes and found myself staring uncomprehendingly at a wholly unfamiliar room.

The décor was gold and deep blue and I discerned immediately that I was in surroundings of luxury and good taste. The bed in which I lay was capacious and comfortable. I somehow knew I had been asleep for many hours. Befuddled, but now wide-awake, I unhurriedly inched myself towards the edge of the bed, got over to it, and forced myself up into a sitting position.

Somewhere I heard the sounds of a television or radio, and all at once it dawned on me that I was in some sort of large suite or apartment. I stood up unsteadily, and as I did so I saw the figure of Vic, now attired in simple slacks, shirt, and loosened tie appear in the bedroom doorway. He came over and solicitously supported me with one arm until I gained my balance. I saw I was wearing dark blue satin pajamas, not my own, and Vic helped me put on a similarly dark blue bathrobe and handed me a pair of leather slippers, and together we went out into a large sitting room in what proved to be a hotel suite.

It was certainly elegant, fit for a king or a president. There was a dining table that could accommodate six persons, and two balconies looked out over what was this day a gray cityscape with snow coming down heavily outside. A large, mounted flat-screen television was on, and I could see that it was airing news coverage of an event apparently of considerable importance. Over on a nearby desk, a laptop was set up and another video stream of the same events, though from a different news source, could be seen. Vic escorted me to a sofa, where I could view the television, and I sat down.

"Coffee, Mr. President?" he asked.

"Yes, thanks," I said. He brought me a cup and sat down nearby.

"Have you got a cigarette on you?" I asked. He tossed me a pack and a book of matches. "Thanks," I said, taking a long draw, "I think I needed that. I seem to be bumming a lot of cigarettes lately."

I gazed at the screen dazedly for a while, sipping the coffee and smoking and regaining as best I could some sense of normality. The news report, I saw, was coming from Rome, and there was a lot of excitement unfolding there—there were rushing vehicles, emergency lights flashing, images of cardinals and bishops in a flurry of overwrought activity, breathless reporters speaking into the cameras, a cascading blur of abrupt interviews, and rolling tickers that kept announcing "Breaking News."

"What's going on?" I asked.

"The pope died last night," said Vic.

"I'm sorry to hear that," I said. "I met him last year. I liked him."

"Died in his sleep," said Vic. "Heart attack, apparently."

"What the hell? You've got to be kidding me."

"No, and that's not all," continued Vic. "The Prefect of the Congregation for the Doctrine of the Faith was found dead in his bedroom this morning with his throat cut. He was a controversial figure, you know."

"Dear God," I said. "That's terrible news." And then I ventured to add, "I know he didn't trust Cardinal Fieropasto."

"I suppose Brother Antoine told you that," said Vic, unfazed by the casual mention of Fieropasto's name. "On the news they're trying to connect the two deaths, but of course they really can't do more than speculate."

And then—as if summoned from the blue—there, on the screen, was Brother Antoine himself. At first I wasn't sure it was he, so altered was his appearance. But, no, it was undeniably he. He was disheveled, cut and bruised as if he had been roughed up, and he was in handcuffs, surrounded by tough-looking Italian police with grim expressions who were hustling him along towards a waiting police vehicle.

"They think he did it. Killed the Prefect, I mean," said Vic.

"Brother Antoine?" I said. "That's ridiculous. I can't imagine him killing anybody."

"He *didn't* kill anybody," replied Vic without emotion. "But you don't need to worry about him. I've fixed it and he'll be cleared and set free soon enough. He just happened to be in the wrong place at the wrong time, which was, of course, Fieropasto's plan."

"Fieropasto?" I asked, beginning to comprehend something of the situation. "*He* was involved...?"

"Antoine will be released in a few hours," Vic went on. "Snithering killed the Prefect, by the way. And also the pope."

"Snithering?" I gasped. "You mean Snithering is a sort of— I don't know what—hit man for Fieropasto?" I realized I was no longer surprised by anything.

"He was in MI6 for a few years," replied Vic. "Did some nasty stuff for them. The only reason he joined the Church was to assuage his conscience. Fieropasto assuaged it for him in exchange for some help in his own intrigues. He slit the Prefect's throat last night, planted the razor in Antoine's room at the Vatican, slipped into the papal apartments—he's a sly customer, a skilled assassin—and injected the pope with potassium chloride. It induces cardiac arrest and it's virtually undetectable, especially in a clumsily organized place like the papal precincts."

"Appalling," I said, still watching the frenetic activities on-screen.

Brother Antoine had been hauled away, and now they were interviewing various high-level prelates.

"He's done it before," said Vic. "Fieropasto, I mean. You may remember what happened in 1978. Snithering did that one, too. A nice touch of theater was included for it, by the way. The newly elected pope died after only thirty-three days. It amused Fieropasto to set it up so that his reign lasted no more than one day for each year of Christ's life. He knew the superstitious would make hay of that. And he had it done on September 28th, the eve of the Feast of St. Michael the Archangel, the heavenly guardian of the Church. An ironic touch, that. He's always had a macabre sense of humor. He invented cutthroat intrigue. He also cooked up the idea of having Leo X assassinated with a poisoned knife while the old boy was being operated on for hemorrhoids. When it comes to style, Fieropasto is actually your model mafioso."

"But, why?" I asked.

"Why the style?"

"No, no. I mean, why the murders?"

"He's always got his reasons. This time it was so he could put his best boy on the papal throne. Someone who'd be your staunch supporter in the days ahead—but answerable only to him, naturally. That won't happen now."

I felt something like a lump in my stomach, a sense of impending disaster and tragedy. I felt myself to be up against a moral wall. One nagging voice in my mind still wanted to take on the role Fieropasto had prepared for me, but only for the purpose of bringing a swift end to Fieropasto by any means. But another part of me, the wiser part, knew I could never bring down Fieropasto—that I was fooling myself to think I could outwit him. To adopt his predetermined role for me would be to do precisely what he most wanted me to do, whatever my rationale for doing it might be—and I was also left in no doubt that my private motivations would be known to him beforehand anyway. Once in power, bit by bit, when I had grown accustomed to my role as the great arbiter for the cause of global justice, then—I knew myself and my flaws too well now—the "reality," the "necessity," the "inevitability" of maintaining order would convince me to toughen up, return to my so-called senses, to *realpolitik* and to Fieropasto's way. I had already shown myself capable of falling to that level. I might, illogically believing in my own strength, be weak enough to do it again. The pictorial evidence in Fieropasto's museum had exposed me as guilty of abominable acts, and nevermore did I want more shed blood on my conscience.

And, then, there was the mountaintop experience—had it been a dream or reality?—and the voice of Vic telling me to get out and that other, more enthralling voice telling me I had no predestined role to fulfill, and that I could never make things better as a ruler in this world, only worse for countless others. There was, when all was said and done, no point or meaning in taking up Fieropasto's offer at all. I was better off disappearing. It shouldn't require the loss of my life—my soul—to try to gain the whole world. It wasn't my place, regardless of my life's preparation for it. In fact, I was beginning to believe, it wasn't anyone's place.

"And the Prefect of the CDF?" I asked. "Why was he killed?"

"He was becoming a thorn in Fieropasto's side, and Antoine's spying—well, there was a score to settle. They knew all about it, you see. Things don't get past Fieropasto for long. Poor Antoine. It was an act of revenge for Snithering, too. He'd been betrayed."

And what will happen to Snithering?" I asked.

"An accident," said Vic. "We all reach the end of the line sooner or later. He'll reach it in a car sometime tonight."

"And Fieropasto?"

"When he realizes he's been set up and the game's over, he'll take off again—as he's always done."

"I see." I finished my cigarette, got up and walked over to the doors that led out onto one of the balconies and watched through the glass panes as the snow came tumbling down from the slate-gray sky.

"Where are we?" I asked.

"The street below is Karl Johans Gate," replied Vic. "We're in the Nobel Suite at the Grand Hotel in Oslo. The date is December 9th, and it's morning. You've been unconscious for days. I brought you here myself, with some help, of course. I told the reporters you were suffering from exhaustion, but you'd be up and ready in time for your big day. They're all out there now—the news media—all wanting a piece of you. The weather's been bad and it's kept down the number of the crowd a bit, but still there are plenty of people out there waiting to see you. You're scheduled to receive the Nobel Peace Prize tomorrow, and it's there that Fieropasto expects you to propose your plan to step into the role he's set up for you. Here's the speech he's written for you, in fact." And Vic picked up a folder from a small side table by the sofa and held it out to me.

I didn't take it and he set it back down. I could see below a gathering of people, the news reporters and cameramen, and a large number of barricading uniformed security forces. I could see that thousands, in fact, were amassed up and down Karl Johans Gate. I knew from experience that many more security personnel, some in SWAT gear, some in plainclothes, were no doubt stationed all around out there, rifles and missile launchers at the ready in case of assassination attempts from below or above. Overhead I could hear the sound of circling helicopters. I glanced upward and they were just barely visible through the snowfall. This is like New York all over again, I thought.

"Tell me, Vic," I said. "And be honest. Who are you? Really, I mean."

"You're an old-timey movie buff and you've watched lots of them," he said. "Especially from the '40s. That's my own era, by the way. I'll tell you what I am—*who* isn't so important. I'm the Clarence to your George Bailey. Get it? The Dudley to your bishop's wife—well, in a manner of speaking, that is. You get me now? I'm running out of comparisons here…"

"As in *It's a Wonderful Life?*" I said at last.

"And *The Bishop's Wife*," he said. "Or, if you prefer scripture to Hollywood, have you read the book of Tobit?"

"It's in the Apocrypha," I said. "I read it once, maybe."

"It's a great little story," said Vic. "Fictional, of course, just like *It's a Wonderful Life* and *The Bishop's Wife*. Maybe you know the gist of it. There's this old guy named Tobit, and one day a pigeon takes a dump on his eyeballs, and the old guy goes blind. But it's okay, because he's got a son—Tobias. Tobias can make a journey on his behalf and work out some things that need working out. Along the way, Tobias runs into his future wife, Sara. She's in trouble. A demon has been killing her husbands one after another. So the two of them pray. Old Man Tobit gets his eyesight back, and Sara gets the demon off her back so she can stop worrying about dead husbands piling up."

"Okay," I said, still looking out at the snow and the bustling crowds and hearing now, as if for the first time, just how loud it all was.

"Remember who helped them out?" Vic continued. "An angel named Raphael. He goes on the trip with Tobias, has all the answers to their problems, and only at the end reveals his secret identity."

I turned from the window and looked Vic in the face. "So, what you're telling me is that you're an angel," I said. "Like Raphael and Clarence and... and..."

"Dudley," said Vic.

"Dudley," I repeated.

"Played by Cary Grant," said Vic.

"Cary Grant," I repeated. "I see for you they could only get Abe Vigoda. Getting back to Clarence, wasn't he supposed to have been a mortal who'd died...?"

"Dudley, too, but of course they're fictional characters," said Vic. "Let's not get too hung up on Hollywood films or the details of Bible stories or archaic terms. 'Angel,' after all, is a pretty ambiguous word. But I *did* admit that the 1940s were really—once upon a time—*my* era..." For a brief instant he looked to me to be a little melancholy.

"But you're not fictional."

"Well, I'm here for you and you can trust me about that," he said simply and then he smiled. "Of course, I say you can trust me, but on the other hand I've deceived you for quite some years now and I bullied you some down in Fieropasto's underworld. You have every reason *not* to trust me and I wouldn't blame you if you didn't right away. But from now on, I'll be as straightforward with you as I can. In the book of Tobit, Raphael lied in a good cause, telling Tobias he was a relative when he really wasn't. Likewise, I had no choice but to deceive you with my series of fake identities. It was really the best way to get you to where you could see the truth."

"Vic," I said, putting my hand on his shoulder, "those were really implausible identities. Anyway, what's going to happen now?"

"That's really up to you," said Vic. "You have your destiny, your responsibility. The world awaits you. And the Norwegian royal family is looking forward to meeting you."

"And Fieropasto has prepared a place for me," I said.

"Everything in your life has brought you to this moment,"

said Vic. "It's who you thought you were before now. Your identity—but, trust me, identities change. I should know. The one constant in life is the ability to change, if you'll pardon the cliché."

I heard the helicopters swooping, humming, chopping, roaring overhead, I heard the noise of excited jabbering voices on the television behind us, and I saw the crowds massing and packed together below, hoping to catch a glimpse of me, perhaps to snap photographs of me with their digital cameras and phones—"like sheep without a shepherd," the phrase went through my head—

—and I woke up fully then and I knew I was never going to be that shepherd.

The time had come for me to step into the role for which I had lived my life thus far.

I also knew I'd just as soon hang myself.

A new determination revitalized me. The world didn't need me, but I needed to have my life before I let it slip through my fingers once and for all. I had already forfeited enough of it. As for Fieropasto—well, he would have to answer, not to me, but to someone who could handle him.

So I said: "Can you get me the hell out of here, Vic, without anyone knowing?"

"You're going to disappoint the King of Norway," he said.

"Please send him my sincerest regrets."

"It's okay. He's used to disappointments. He eats lutefisk on Christmas. Which is coming up soon, by the way. Not the lutefisk. Christmas. How would you like to celebrate it somewhere else than New York? Anyway, yes. I can get you out of here."

"Perhaps to a mountain to raise goats."

He smiled at me—and I knew he knew, and that it was only a matter of who had been doing the dreaming all along. Somewhere the Red King was slumbering.

"Don't be a literalist," he said. "I know a place where you

won't be disturbed and can live out all your remaining years without pretense, making reparation for your past. A place where you can be awake, alert, and focused on what really matters before you die. And you can learn how to do what's really good—good for others. Goats don't enter into it. And I'll be sure to drop in on you from time to time to see how you are, and maybe I'll even bring you some scotch and some decent cigars."

"And can you send a message to Fieropasto for me?" I asked.

"I can arrange it," he replied.

"Then tell him," I said, "that I have better things to do than run the world and try to fix it. Tell him I intend to dip my feet in mountain streams, toss pebbles, listen to birds, watch clouds, and learn to shut up and pray. Tell him I reject privilege and the spotlight. Tell him I think Jesus was right. Tell him I walk away from it all and won't be looking back. And also tell him that, under no circumstances, is he ever to bother me again. Not even a phone call or a birthday card. That's all."

Vic pulled two cigars from his shirt pocket. "I've been saving these for the right occasion," he said, handing me one. He struck a match, held it out, and, as he lit my cigar, he said, "That message to Fieropasto—it's as good as delivered."

Acknowledgments

IT would be ungrateful not to acknowledge my brother David, whose encouragement led me to consider seeking publication for what was originally only a diversion for me. I regret that my mother, who so enjoyed the first draft of this story a decade ago, didn't live to see it in print. Most of all, I'm grateful to my son, Addison, who is a skillful editor in his own right. He read through the manuscript more than once and made copious suggestions, most of which I used. Lastly, I'm grateful to the publisher for taking a chance with this strange concoction.

Made in the USA
Middletown, DE
06 March 2020